Rhett Redeemed includes brief, non-explicit references to the shooting of a child, as well as unrelated child death.

RHETT REDEEMED

CHANTAL FERNANDO

carina
press

carina
press®

Recycling programs
for this product may
not exist in your area.

ISBN-13: 978-1-335-53000-4

Rhett Redeemed

For questions and comments about the quality of this book, please contact us at CustomerService@Harlequin.com.

Carina Press
22 Adelaide St. West, 41st Floor
Toronto, Ontario M5H 4E3, Canada
www.CarinaPress.com

Printed in U.S.A.

For Amo.

Your loyalty, understanding and
deep soul deserve their own mention.

Thank you for making me feel
accepted, and seen.

(And for supporting me
as I come out as a Slytherin.)

I love you and all your darkness.

RHETT REDEEMED

"Tell me every terrible thing you ever did, and let me love you anyway."

—Sade Andria Zabala

Prologue

Con

The last few months of my life have been a complete whirlwind. I feel like I've forgotten who I am. Like I've been going through the motions of life, but really, deep inside I'm flailing.

Falling.

Lost.

I rest my hands against my flat stomach, my eyes closed and my mind trying to process everything that has happened.

I don't know how I got here. I don't know how every decision I made led me to this moment. But I'm here. And now I'm going to have to face the music.

Because I'm pregnant.

And the father?

My sister's ex-boyfriend.

Chapter One

Con

There has to be more to life than this.

Work and home, home and work—the daily grind and routine has me caught in a rut. I'm alive, but I'm not living.

There's nothing like working hard every single day and still only barely getting by to ruin your morale. And for what? Only to go home alone, and then do it all over again the next day.

"Table six is still waiting," says my boss, Max, impatience filling his tone as he breaks me out of my pity party.

"I know," I reply absently. "I'm on it." I say that as I continue to wait for the food. There's not much I can do if the food isn't ready.

As I watch Max flit around to nag another waitress, my mind wanders back to when my father was alive. When I was in college and living my best life. Don't get me wrong, my father was not the best dad. He wasn't even worthy of an honorable mention. But he did what he could. He paid for college, at least, and tried to make sure I had what I needed to find success in life. I can't exactly say we had a close bond either, but my mom used to always say, "You only get one father," and it stuck, especially after she passed away.

Now that he's gone, I'm glad we tried. But here I am six months later, a college dropout with a full-time waitressing job to pay the mortgage on his house so I can have a place to live.

Did I get the shit-end of the stick?

Probably.

But when you lose your mom and then your dad, and a house full of memories is all you have left of them, you hold on to that. Even if the memories aren't always the best ones.

So now I'm here wondering what the hell I'm doing with my life. I haven't always made the best decisions, and at some point, I need to find a better path. Basically, I need to stop being a hot mess.

Yes, I'm kind of alone in the world, but this is my life.

And it's up to me to make some changes to make it better.

I have to be the hero I need right now instead of sitting around waiting for him to stroll in.

Because he isn't coming.

The food for table six finally arrives and I carry it out, a plate in each hand, and place it down on the table. "Sorry for the wait—here is your steak and seafood chowder."

I pick up the table number as the two gentlemen thank me, and then head over to wait on two men who have just walked in and sat at table eight. They're both bikers, going by their leather cuts—we get quite a few of them in here.

I pull out my notebook and glance between the two of them. They are both good-looking, and give off vibes that they know it, but the blond man instantly catches my eye, his blue eyes scanning the menu and then looking up at me. He exudes power, and recklessness, and apparently I'm drawn to that. Who knew? I normally go for the average Joe—decent looking, decent job. I find that if you don't set my expectations too high, I'm less likely to be disappointed.

But this one definitely catches my eye.

"I'll have a black coffee. And the ribs, please," Blond Guy says, placing the menu down and leaning back in the booth. I don't miss the slow perusal he gives me, checking me out from head to toe, but I pretend that I do. Being a waitress, I get hit on all of the time, and I certainly have found that ignoring it is the best way to handle it. If you flirt, you can get more tips, but I tried that and it's just not for me. I just try to be polite and work hard, and hope that's enough. We already have to wear tight tops to work, as requested by Max, and even though we just work in the restaurant, we get treated the same as the women who strip at Toxic next door.

Some men just seem to think we are free game.

"Dice?" Blond Guy prompts his friend, a red-haired man.

"Ummm. I'll have the nachos and a beer."

"No problem," I reply, picking up the menus and heading back to the kitchen. I slide the order slip to the chefs at the back and get the coffee and beer.

"Damn, want to swap tables?" Jamie asks me, checking out the bikers. Jamie has been working here longer than me, and was the one to show me the ropes when I first started. She's a fun, bubbly blonde and is always the one who gets the most tips. She's stunning, with an infectious personality, so I can see why.

"If you want," I reply with a shrug. We get good-looking men coming in here all the time; it's all the same to me. Although something about the blond intrigues me, which means I should probably stay away.

She playfully nudges me. "You all right? How did it go seeing your sister the other day?"

I perk up at the mention of Cara, my half sister who I recently met for the first time. "It was good. We went out for dinner and a movie. It's been great getting to know her."

In reality, it's been an emotional roller coaster.

While going through my father's stuff after his death, I found out about Cara. Dad pretty much had no involvement in Cara's life, which is probably why I never heard of her, but I was angry at him for not telling me I had an older sister. I've always felt so alone, and to know I have a sister out there excited me. After I hired a PI to find her, she and I met and the rest is history.

Cara is everything I'm not. She's educated, classy and extremely put together. She's assertive, and strong, yet also sweet and kind.

And she's happy.

Me? I'm all over the place. I don't have a career, I'm a little rough around the edges and I didn't have two loving parents like she did. I pretty much raised myself, while Cara grew up in a loving, supportive home.

We aren't the same.

But despite what anyone thinks, I have nothing but genuine love for Cara. I'm not envious of her; I want her to have all of that and more. Having her in my life has given me a connection that my existence has been lacking. She's a special person, and I can see why she has so many people that adore her.

"That's nice. You'll have to bring her in one day so we can all meet her," Jamie replies, smiling at me.

"I will," I promise. "You want to take these out to them?"

She nods, taking the tray. I watch her strut over and bend over the table in her short-shorts, laughing at something one of them has said. I notice the blond one looking over at me, our eyes meeting over the back of Jamie's shapely ass.

Looking away, I start drying the glasses and keeping myself busy. I need to figure out what I want to do with my life. I don't want to work here forever. Not that there's anything wrong with being a waitress—a job is a job—but I know this isn't where I want to be forever. I want to be able to work toward something, at least. I need something positive in my life.

"What are you thinking about?" Jamie asks as she's coming back from the table, breaking me out from my trance.

"Just contemplating my life," I admit.

"Here," she says, handing me the plates of food for the biker men. "You take these out to the hot bikers and then have your break. The hot one was asking about you, and you look like you need a sneaky shot of tequila."

He was asking about me? Why?

She heads off to serve the new customers who walk in, and I bring the food over to the bikers. "Your ribs," I say, as I place the plate down in front of the blond. "And the nachos," to his friend. "Is there anything else I can get you?"

"No, thank you," the blond replies, studying me. "Except maybe your number."

My eyebrows raise. "Not on the menu, unfortunately. Enjoy the rest of your evening."

I flash him a smile, and then head back to the kitchen, hearing his deep laugh behind me. I have enough problems in my life right now; I don't need any more. And he has trouble written all over him. Delicious, orgasm-attached trouble, but trouble nonetheless.

I take Jamie's advice, down a shot of tequila, and then eat some garlic bread for my dinner. Because why the fuck not.

Jamie pokes her head in. "Hot biker left this for you." She hands me a piece of paper with his number on it. "You going to text him? You should. He's sexy."

I shake my head, scrunch up the paper and throw it across the room into the trash like it's a basketball hoop. "Nope."

She frowns, resting her hand on her hip. "No harm in getting some di—"

"Jamie, get out here!" Max calls, and she rolls her eyes and heads back to work.

I dust the crumbs off my black pants and mentally prepare myself for another four hours of work. I don't need to be thinking about the sexy biker, I need to be thinking about how I'm going to get out of this rut that I'm in.

I get a text message from Cara.

Cara: You said you wanted to find a new job, right?

When we went out the other night, I told her that I wasn't loving it here anymore, and that I'd started to look for something new. She must have really listened to what I was saying.

Con: Yes? Why?

Cara: You open to anything? Like working in a custom motorcycle garage?

My fingers pause over the keyboard. I don't know anything about custom motorcycles, but I'm a fast learner, and I can't afford to be picky. Any change is a good change right now, I know that my mental health needs it, and this could be a good opportunity for me, the one that I've been wanting.

Con: Yes please. Just at work now, I'll text you later.

I put my phone away and head out to serve more customers, smiling to myself that Cara is looking out for me. It feels so damn good to finally have someone on my side, on my team.

I always wanted a big sister, and although we met late, it looks like I was blessed with a good one.

Chapter Two

Rhett

About a year ago, I had a choice to make. An impossible choice.

Arrow, the Wind Dragons president; Sin, the former president; and Talon, my stepdad, all sat me down to let me know they wanted me to become the next Wind Dragons president when Arrow was ready to retire. While this is something that had been talked about in passing, I never really thought it was real until I heard the words out of Arrow's mouth.

"You're next up."

And I fucking wanted it. The idea that I would become the leader of the fiercest motorcycle club was a dream come true. You know how when you're little and people ask you what you want to be when you grow up? Truth is I never had an answer other than "provide for my mother." But once the Wind Dragons came into my life when I was a kid, it was all I ever saw for myself. Wearing a cut, riding a motorcycle. That was the dream.

And having Cara by my side and on the back of my

bike. I don't think either of us saw anything different for ourselves.

Until our best friend, Clover, was threatened and Cara and I had to go hide out or risk being killed.

That changed a lot of things for Cara.

"What does that entail exactly?" I had asked. I mean, I know we see Arrow leading, making decisions and generally handling shit, but what exactly comes with being a president?

"You will lead the MC, you will be responsible for all of the members and the various businesses and you will uphold the legacy of the Wind Dragons," Arrow had replied. "You will still have us to guide you, but being president will consume you. Your MC will be your life."

"The MC is my life now," I'd said.

Sin had shaken his head. "It's a heavy burden, being responsible for everything. Making all decisions and dealing with the consequences that come with them. You'll also be responsible for making sure we're making money with the businesses. Being the president and not just a member is a whole different ball game. People will target you. You need to watch your back at all times. It's a war out there, Rhett. Do you think you can handle all of that?"

I had nodded, but the conversation with them had me concerned. Why did they sound like they were warning me? They both did it, so I could too, right?

Clover, Cara and I had grown up seeing everything Clover's mother, Faye, went through as Sin's old lady, and then watched Anna and Arrow navigate it as well. They each had been put through hell and back, and now that was going to be Cara's life. That was the life I was giving her.

That was when I knew I loved her too much to ask that of her.

So I made a choice.

And that choice brought me to here, to right now.

"What are you thinking about so deeply?" Sin asks, breaking me from my thoughts. He sits down next to me on the couch, beer in hand. The clubhouse is all of our homes, and it always has been my happy place.

"I was thinking about the time you all told me I was going to be the next president," I admit. "I remember feeling like it was a warning."

"It was," Sin replies, smirking. "Being president isn't for the faint of heart. We wanted to make sure that we were making the right decision."

"And did you?"

He takes a swig of the beer before answering. "I think so, but only time will tell. Are you regretting the decision?"

I shake my head. "No…but I feel like I'm already making sacrifices and I'm not even officially president yet."

"Ah… Cara?"

I give a stiff nod.

"Have you spoken to her yet?"

I shake my head.

"You should. The two of you have a bond, and you need to repair it, even if its form has changed. She'll forgive you eventually."

"I know."

And I will.

When I'm ready.

* * *

"How have you been?" Dad asks, sipping on his whiskey. He found me at my go-to bar, and I know he just wants to see where I'm at mentally right now. Sin must've said something to him.

"I'm okay," I lie.

The truth is, I'm struggling.

I've never experienced the gut-wrenching pain from a breakup before. Cara has been my only committed relationship, and although I've had plenty of other women, she's the only one I have ever called mine. The pain from losing her, even if it was my own choices that led to that decision, is more than I could have imagined.

I think the hardest part of it all is that she was more than just my lover—she was my best friend. And although we promised to try to maintain that friendship, I know things will never be the same.

And that's on me and my decision not to tell her the truth and give her a choice.

I can only blame my damn self.

And no amount of alcohol and women is making it better, and trust me, I have tried. I've been spending my newfound single status fucking any woman who wants to, and drinking as much as I can. I know that the Wind Dragons are unimpressed with me. I'm supposed to be taking over and leading a new generation of Wind Dragons, letting the older, OG men retire. Yet here I am, partying and fucking and forgetting my responsibilities, the same ones I let go of Cara for. How fucking ironic. But Cara was my home, and now I'm homeless.

I rub my chest, over my heart, like I can physically feel the damage I've done to my vital organ.

But you know what? Cara deserves more. She deserves someone who comes home to her every night, someone who can make her his number one priority. Someone who can give her the life that she wants.

She deserves everything I can't give her.

She might have grown up in this life, but that doesn't mean that's what she wants her future to be.

I've contemplated going after her m⁰s, begging for her to take me back, but she's happy now, and I'm not going to be selfish. This all happened for a reason, and I know it will be the right one for both of us.

I see the way she looks at Decker; it's the way she used to look at me. A mix of awe, admiration and unconditional love.

I pick up another shot of tequila and let it roll down my throat. The thought of her with another man still makes me want to punch something. But this is my new reality, and I need to accept it and be happy for her.

It's just a little harder than I had imagined it would be.

"It's been three months, Rhett," my father says from beside me. Technically Talon is my stepfather, but just like Cara, I was adopted into the Wind Dragons family when my mom, Tia, fell in love with a biker. Talon was actually the president of another MC before leaving and joining the Wind Dragons. Unlike Cara, though, I've always known this was my world, and instead of stepping away from it, I've only fallen deeper.

He rests his hand on my shoulder and gives it a squeeze. "You need to focus if you still want to take over from Arrow. Everyone is watching you."

"I know," I admit, nodding in agreement. "I'll be fine. I'll be ready."

I don't even sound that sure to my own ears. I knew losing her was going to hurt, but I didn't know it was going to fuck me up this badly.

"I know you loved Cara, son, but it's time to move forward now."

Loved.

Past tense.

I guess that's how we're all going to be speaking about her now.

"Sometimes your first love isn't the person you are meant to be with. That doesn't mean there isn't someone out there for you," he says, taking a sip of his own drink and placing the glass back down. "Your soul mate is still out there. But right now, you have other things you need to be focused on."

"How do you know she wasn't my soul mate and that I just fucked it up?" I ask, jaw tensing.

"If she was, she wouldn't have fallen in love with another man so soon," he says bluntly, wincing as he delivers that blow. "Sorry, son, but it's true."

That hurts more than getting physically hit.

"I know you both loved each other, but things don't always work out, Rhett. Life throws you all kinds of curveballs. You need to accept it for what is it and move on. We all love Cara, but you cheated on her. You made your choice, and now she has made hers, and you need to respect that."

"I have accepted it, otherwise I'd be at her house banging on the door begging for her to take me back."

"Okay, good. Prez has a meeting tomorrow, and he wants you to be there."

"I'll be there," I promise. Likely hungover, but I'll still be there.

"Okay," he murmurs, studying me for a few seconds. "Your mom is worried about you."

"I'll come see her tomorrow, too."

He nods and then leaves the bar, letting me return to my pity party. I order another drink and scan the crowd, a pretty brunette catching my eye. A simple smile and she makes her way over to me.

Maybe this is my life now—meaningless sex and alcohol on repeat.

Anything that distracts me.

I buy her a drink, finish mine, and then she takes me back to her house.

And the most fucked-up thing? When I come, I mouth a name that's not hers.

"Looks like I arrived just in time," I say in greeting, taking solace in my mom's warm embrace.

"How are you?" she asks, looking up at me with concern etched on her face.

"I'm okay," I reply, kissing the top of her head. I hate that she has been worrying about me. I know she didn't necessarily want me to follow in Talon's footsteps—she had a different vision of me going to college and getting a degree instead of becoming a biker. But she made this world our own, so she can't hold it against me. "I thought I'd drop in and say hello before I head to the clubhouse."

She turns off the stove and starts fixing our plates.

"I'm glad you did. I tried calling you yesterday and when you didn't answer, I was worried."

"I know, Mom. I was out with Dice and then I forgot to call you back," I explain as I sit down at the breakfast bar. Dice only just got patched in this month, but he's a pretty cool dude. He's levelheaded, loyal, and I've grown to trust him. Every time I've needed him, he has come through, and I know he's going to be at my side when I become president. We have several other prospects waiting to be patched in, and these are the men who will help me carry on the Wind Dragons legacy.

Over the last year, Arrow has had me there the entire way, helping choose who I want to be a part of the MC. I have a lot of pressure on me to be the man the MC needs, and it's hard to do that with my own personal life going to hell. But I've always lived and breathed the MC, from back when I would watch my dad come home wearing his Wind Dragons cut. I knew this is where I wanted to be, and now it's the only thing I have left.

She places a plate down and sits next to me. "Cara came over yesterday and we had a big talk. That's why I called you."

I freeze. "What did she say?"

No one knows the truth about my decision with Cara. That I didn't cheat on her. That I couldn't even think about sleeping with another woman.

I mean, I did let Trisha kiss me at the club, so there is that. But it's only because I knew Cara was there and that if I was going to follow through with my plan, she'd have to see it to believe it. Trisha may have kissed me unexpectedly, but I couldn't have planned a more perfect time. I saw Cara see me and I purposefully didn't push Trisha away. But I hated the kiss. And thinking back on it, I'm fucking ashamed that I did that instead of talking to Cara and being honest with her about our relationship.

I know Cara, though. She's loyal, and she would have fought for us. But I knew she wouldn't fight for someone she thought had betrayed her. I knew that, and I used it against her. Who does that to a good woman? A coward—that's who. I'm well aware that if I told someone the truth, especially my mom, she would've talked me out of it.

"Nothing, just that she promised to continue to come around and that you and her are in a good place despite the circumstances."

Typical Cara, not saying a bad word against me. Mom loves Cara, always has ever since she was a child. I know this whole breakup has to be hard on her, too.

"I'm sorry, Mom. I know you love Cara like your own daughter."

My mom and Cara's mom, Bailey, were neighbors, and became best friends even before the Wind Dragons entered any of our lives. This is so much more than a normal breakup. Our whole lives and families are intertwined. Another thing I failed to think about when I put this plan into action.

"Don't be sorry. Maybe it just wasn't meant to be," she replies, forcing a sad smile. "But we never did talk about what happened."

I stop eating my eggs and look up at her in surprise. "What do you mean? You know what happened. Cara fell in love with some ex-cop." Yes, I'm putting the blame on Cara here, but this is my mom, and if there is one person I should still have on my side, it's her. Besides, what could there possibly be left to talk about?

"Rhett, honey, there has to be more to this story. You always loved Cara, you'd do anything for her. I don't see how you could let her go like that…"

I'm thankful in this moment that no one has told my mom why Cara and I broke up. If my mother were to think of me as a cheater, it would hurt almost as much as it hurts to see Cara with another man. I don't really care what the guys think, but the last thing I want is for my mother to look at me with disappointment in her eyes. There's no way Mom would be okay with me treating any woman like that, and especially not Cara. She would be telling me that she raised me better than that.

"Mom, it wasn't meant to be. There is nothing left to talk about." I orchestrated my own heartbreak because I'm a selfish fuck. End of story.

"But Cara says that you're being supportive of her new relationship and that you handled it well…"

This makes me feel even worse. They say a person's true character is shown when you break up with them, and Cara is just further proving she has a heart of gold. I mean, if I ignore the whole moving-on-so-quickly thing, that is. Yes, she has every right to fall in love, but did it have to be so soon after we broke up? I never once thought that she would do that.

But hey, maybe I never really knew her at all.

And maybe she never really knew me at all. Because if she did, she'd have known I never would have been unfaithful to her. But she believed it, and I let her.

And now it's both of our realities.

"Yeah, Mom, I'm doing super."

I give her a kiss and head to the clubhouse, the only thing I have left in this world.

Chapter Three

Con

The next night after our shift, Jamie convinces me to head out for a few drinks. We go back to my house and get changed first, and then go barhopping. We have a cocktail at every venue we stop at, which is kind of fun, but also probably not very smart because we are mixing drinks.

"This one is the best one so far," I say after another sip of the espresso martini. "It's delicious."

Jamie nods in agreement, pressing her pink lips together. "It's good. Strong, though."

"Exactly." I grin, taking another mouthful. Maybe I'm at the stage where everything tastes good. "I'm glad you convinced me to come out tonight," I admit, placing my empty cocktail glass on the bar and turning to face her. "I think I needed it."

"I think so, too. You've been so stressed out and… brooding."

She's right, I have been extremely stressed out, and just not feeling like myself. I'd never admit it out loud, but maybe seeing everything Cara has is making me

realize how little I have. And I'm not talking about material things. I'm talking about a life filled with love,
surrounded by quality people and security. I have none
of those things. Yeah, Jamie is a good friend, but she's
not my best friend. I'm just one of her many friends. I
don't have anyone in my life who would put me first.
I'm no one's favorite person. And that realization was
hard to come to when I saw Cara with her boyfriend,
Decker, and her best friend, Clover.

And on that thought… "Could I please have two wet
pussy shots and two more of these martinis?" I ask the
bartender, pulling my chestnut-colored hair in a bun to
keep it out of my face.

"Damn, girl," Jamie mutters, knowing how drunk
we are about to be at the end of this night.

I open my handbag and search for my debit card
when a muscled arm drops some cash on the bar in
front of me. I glance up from his fingers to his forearm, the veins in his arm catching my eye. I don't know
why, but I've always found those attractive in men, and
my gaze keeps going upward until my eyes are locked
with blue ones.

"I got it." Shoulder-length blond hair, worn down and
around his chin, stubble on his jaw and a confidence I
find dangerous.

The blond biker from the restaurant last night. The
sexy one who gave me his number, the number that I
threw out right after.

"I can pay for my own drinks," I mutter, pursing my
red-tinted lips.

The weird thing is, I actually had a dream about this
man last night. An explicit one. I woke up horny as hell,

and now he's standing in front of me in all of his tall, leather-clad glory.

"I remember you!" Jamie says and, unlike me, smiles warmly. She nudges me. "Say hello. And thank you for the drinks."

"No problem," he replies, amused.

Our drinks arrive, and I realize he paid for ours but didn't get himself anything, so I awkwardly offer him my shot. "Wet pussy?"

"I'd love one." He smirks, taking the shot from me and downing it. "That's...sweet."

"Yes, it is."

Jamie glances between him and me, and then does her own shot. "I'm going to go and have a dance. I'll be where I can see you."

She leaves with a wave of her fingers and makes friends on the dance floor with a bunch of women who easily accept her. If I walked over, I don't think I'd get the same reception. Jamie is just a likable person with a good energy about her. But me? I have my walls up, and people can usually sense that and leave me alone. Most take it as me being a bitch, but I think I do it to protect myself from rejection. Where is Dr. Phil? I'm standing in front of a gorgeous guy and here I am still having my pity party.

"You never texted me," he points out.

"I did not." I snap out of my funk. *Head in the game, Con.* "That unusual for you?"

I study his beautiful blue eyes. When I look at him I see a kindred soul. I recognize the loneliness in his eyes—it's the same loneliness I see in my own reflection.

He runs his hand over his blond hair as his lip twitches. "I just felt an attraction between us. Maybe it was one-sided." He turns to face the dance floor with his elbows leaning against the bar.

It definitely wasn't. Even now, being so close to him, my nipples are hard as ice. I find myself gravitating closer to him until our arms graze and it feels like an injection into my blood stream. Or maybe it's the alcohol. Either way, the sexual chemistry is there all right.

"Not every attraction needs to be acted upon," I say, looking at him from the side.

He turns to me, which is startling at first. His blue gaze scans mine. "True. But there's something about you. Do you want to dance?"

A dance couldn't hurt, right?

I shrug, and he walks backward to the dance floor, offering me his hand. I take it and a zap of electricity goes up my arm. It's as if I feel a jolt for the first time in a long while.

And I have an epiphany.

In this moment, I'm free.

I feel *something*.

And it's been so long since I have felt anything, I'm only realizing that right now. I've just been breathing, but not living.

I let him guide me, stopping next to Jamie and her new squad and starting to move to the beat. I'm a little stiff at the start, but when I relax, I get into the music and enjoy myself. I even find myself smiling with him, the two of us close, but not so close that we are touching. He keeps a safe distance, and I respect that.

I make the first move by closing the space between

us and pressing my body up against his. His eyes widen ever so slightly, and he's probably wondering why I've decided to be so bold, especially since I turned him down yesterday.

I'm wondering the same thing. But I'm sure I'm just another notch on his belt, so why not allow myself to have a little pleasure? Live a little.

This feeling that I'm having, I don't want it to stop.

Besides, good sex seems like a distant memory. Maybe that's why I'm so tense these days. My vibrator might make me come, but it doesn't give me a connection with another person. And that is what my life is seriously lacking.

We continue to dance for a few more songs, and I find myself letting loose and letting go. He leaves the dance floor and comes back with two bottles of water, and I thank him and drink greedily. He watches me as I lick the water off my lips. Our eyes connect and hold, and I can't deny the heat there. My gaze drops to his lips, and I find myself wondering how they taste.

"You're so sexy," he whispers into my ear, hand on the side of my neck, his lips brushing my skin, sending shivers down my spine. He kisses my neck, but stops to look at me, silently asking for my permission.

He wants me. And fuck it… I want him, too.

I give him a small nod and he goes over to Jamie to say something to her. I'm not sure what it is until I see her saying goodbye to the group of ladies she met on the dance floor. I guess we're leaving.

We get in a waiting cab and drop Jamie off first. "Text me," she says with wide eyes as she gets out.

I nod. "I will."

"Look after her," she tells him, who promises that he will. It's in that moment that I realize I don't even know his name. I should be concerned, scared even, but there is something alluring to the anonymity. To not knowing each other's names.

Then it's just me and him in the back of the vehicle, our shoulders and fingers touching, the tension between us thick. I give the driver my address next, deciding I'd rather go to my home than his to maintain a semblance of control.

I want to jump on him, straddle him and kiss him, but then we'd probably get kicked out of the cab, so instead I just sit here, trying to slow my breathing and wait until we get to my house. It doesn't help when he starts to run his fingers up and down my thigh, and I look straight ahead and wonder if the cabdriver can feel the tension in the car or if it's just me.

When we finally get to my house, Rhett pays the driver and we both get out. I dig the house key out of my bag, but before I can even put it in the door, he's on me, lifting me up against the wall, and we're both kissing frantically. My hair is everywhere, falling on my face, and when he tries to push it out of the way, the keys fall from my hand and onto the floor. I'm so wet that he could just fuck me right now for the world to see without any other foreplay.

"Get the keys," I command as he starts to kiss down my neck.

With me still in his arms, he bends down and grabs the keys, unlocks the door and lets us both inside.

"Where's your room?" he asks, tone deep and husky. "Never mind, we aren't going to make it."

I've never felt more relief than I do at that moment.

He finds the living room, throws me down onto the couch and starts kissing me. I grab him by the pants and begin taking his belt off with clumsy fingers. He eventually does it for me, stripping down naked while I pull off my dress, leaving me in heels and a black bra and panties.

He sits back and I do to him what I wanted to in the cab, straddling him and kissing him while his hands cup the globes of my ass. He's rock hard, and without thinking I slide my panties to the side, place his cock against my pussy and push down. He moans, and it's sexy as hell and turns me on even more. I was right—no foreplay needed.

I ride him fast and hard, and then he switches positions, laying me down on my stomach with my ass up in the air. He slides back and enters me from behind, with me pushing against him, meeting him thrust for thrust.

"Fuck," he grits out, reaching between my thighs and stroking my clit. He makes me come in no time, and when I'm done I think he's going to pound away behind me and finish himself off. But instead he rolls me onto my back and goes down on me, making me come again before he slides his cock back in and starts to move inside me again, slowly this time, while staring straight into my eyes.

I've had a few one-night stands in my time, but none of them have been like this. There is a connection here, and I can't seem to put words to it. It's more than a great orgasm.

I don't know what to think, so I don't, I block out my thoughts and just feel.

And it's fucking amazing.

Chapter Four

Rhett

I wake up in the morning and sit up quickly, until I remember where I am. After the couch sex, I ended up in the waitress's bed, where we had another two rounds before falling asleep.

I'm ashamed to admit it, but I've slept with a few women this week. Tonight has to be the best so far.

Shit, I always use protection, I'm religious about it now that Cara and I are broken up, but it completely slipped my mind last night. Fuck fuck fuck. I have to hope that… Shit. I don't even know her name.

I'd never confess it out loud, but at the restaurant, when I first saw this beautiful creature, she kind of reminded me of Cara. I've been purposefully avoiding sleeping with any brunettes to avoid associating anyone with Cara. I obviously got a thing for brunettes, because that seems to be my type. Or is it because Cara is a brunette? I don't know.

But when I saw her at the bar last night, my no-brunettes rule went out the window. There was some heat between her and I, and I'm glad she allowed us to explore it. The sex was phenomenal. It's the first time in however many months that I didn't think of Cara while I was with a woman. I may be a pussy to admit it, but in the past I've had to think of Cara to get myself going with the other women. But with this woman, I didn't think of Cara once. I don't think I could've even if I wanted to. She made me feel alive, even if it was only for the moment.

She surprised me with how sensual and giving she is in bed, and I would definitely fuck her again, given the chance. With protection this time. I realize I should leave before she wakes up and turns the perfect one-night stand into something awkward.

As I head to the door, I see a piece of mail on her table and read her name: Constance Wilder. Wild she is.

I call a cab that takes me back to my place. Once I get home, I take a shower and hop into my own bed. I just rented this house, but no one knows about it aside from the Wind Dragons. Clover and Cara don't even know that I'm in town right now and not miles away, near the clubhouse. After an incident that happened with the street gang the Forgotten Children, aka the FC, I put Cara and Clover in danger, and when that was over, I stuck around to make sure that they were okay. Since then, I've been going back and forth from here and the Wind Dragons clubhouse, which is about a two-hour drive depending on the traffic.

I also own a house with Cara near the clubhouse, one that Cara thinks is being sold, but it's not. It's just sitting there. I know how much she loved that house, and I just can't seem to get rid of it. Maybe I'll keep it for her and she can do with it as she chooses. I just can't be the one to sell it. If she wants to, fine, but I won't do it.

I check my phone, and I don't miss how dry it's been since Cara and I broke up. I know Clover is still disappointed in me, and I know that Cara and I will never be the same, which tears me up inside. This just shows that all those times Cara accused me of being too impulsive and warned that it would get me into trouble, she was right. Once I made up my mind that this was the path I was going to go down, I made sure to be seen talking to women and stopped going home to Cara. By the time I realized the implications of people thinking I was cheating, it was too late to turn back. The damage was already done.

Cara and Clover have been my best friends ever since I can remember. Growing up, the other boys at school thought it was so weird I was so close with them. They even tried to tease me about it.

"How come you're best friends with girls? Are you gay?" one asked me in front of the girls.

I remember sharing a look with Cara and Clover, both such strong girls, even back then. Clover had a big mouth on her and wasn't afraid to use it, whereas Cara was quieter and more reserved, but always had our backs.

"Maybe it's because we have bigger balls than you," Clover had replied to the kid, with a cocky smirk.

The kid got angry and tried to hit her, so of course I stepped in and taught him a lesson. No one hurts my girls.

No one except me, apparently.

I contemplated telling Clover the truth right before everything went down with the Forgotten Children, but then shit hit the fan and I was gone for weeks. By the time I got back and had a chance, everyone had made up their minds about me, and I took the easy way out and let them.

I know this is all my doing, but it still hurts.

I think about the Wind Dragons, where we've been, where we are and where I want to lead us. The club went through so much, with a few of the members doing time behind bars, like Arrow and Irish. But no matter what, they all stayed loyal to each other, and they would go to the end of the earth to protect the extended family they've created.

Am I setting myself up for failure by wanting the same kind of club I grew up around as a kid? A ride-or-die club of men who have each other's backs and have a genuine bond that will never end? I wonder if the men I've surrounded myself with are going to be as loyal to me and the club as past members were. When all of the older generation steps away, what will we have left? And will it be enough? It takes a certain type of man to live and breathe this life, and I hope that kind still exists in the younger members.

I realize that I have no one to speak to about this, no one to confide in. Dad warned me that it would be lonely, being the man in charge, but at the time I didn't really hear what he was saying. Maybe it's not just the Cara thing that has me questioning if I've taken on too much too soon.

But I've come this far and I can't back away now.

If not me, then who?

* * *

"You've been MIA," Arrow comments when he sees me the next day, finally making an appearance at the clubhouse. He's an intimidating man, even when you've known him since you were a kid, like me. He demands respect, and we all give it to him.

"I know," I reply, pulling out the bar stool next to him and sitting down. "Just getting my head right."

Arrow nods. He looks tired, and I feel like shit that I haven't been here, proving to him that the MC will be left in good hands. While there's nothing too big going on with the club at the moment, from experience I know that can change in an instant. Not to mention I'm supposed to be spending time with the prospects, forming a bond with them and weeding out the men I don't want at my back. These are my generation of MC brothers, and I need to make sure I'm surrounded by people I can trust, especially if I want the MC to continue to be strong and resilient.

"I know you're still fucked-up over Cara," he states, swirling the amber liquid in his glass. "Trust me, the first heartbreak is the worst, but as president, you'll need to be strong for the club, no matter what's going on in your own personal life. I talked Rake out of wanting to fight you, so there's that, too. I think you should have a talk with him."

Rake is Cara's dad, an OG member of the club and someone I've always looked up to. He has always been like a second father to me, but I understand why he'd be mad. I respect it, even. If I had a daughter and someone broke her heart, I'd want a piece of him, too.

How many fucking bridges have I burned just because I lied? Too many to count.

But that's not the real reason I don't tell Cara the truth, is it?

No, it's more selfish than that.

I needed to choose between the club and Cara.

Before I jumped headfirst into my ruse, I contemplated giving the club up. But I had nothing to fall back on. I knew nothing else other than the club and I realized I didn't want to know anything else other than the club. The Wind Dragons are my home, just like my mother's house will always be my home. I couldn't give that up even if it meant losing a piece of my heart.

It's pretty fucked-up when I think about it that way. But seeing how happy she is now, I know that I made the right choice, even if it's killing me.

"I will talk to Rake," I promise. I'll continue to be the bad guy, because to be honest, it's an easier role than the truth. "What was it like when Sin stepped down and you took over? How did you keep everyone together? I want us to remain the tight-knit unit that we are known for, but I'm not sure how to do that with all the new people coming in."

Or maybe I just don't know how to do that.

If Arrow is surprised by my question, he doesn't show it. "I think it was easier for me to take over because Sin had it all set up. We knew the men in our club. We trusted each other. They respected me already, and I had already earned their loyalty. And I'm older. With you being younger and having new people patching in, it's going to be more difficult. There will be some curveballs thrown your way. Why are you having doubts? I know you've been partying a lot more recently, so if this is something you don't want anymore, you need to let me know."

With that I look him in the eye and see something I haven't seen in a while—hesitation. Does he think I can't do this? Is he regretting his decision about me?

"Do you not think I can do it?"

He sighs deeply. "We picked you for a reason. We know you can handle it. Shit, more than handle it. But you cannot let yourself get distracted. And you've been distracted."

"I'll get my head on straight. I got this."

"I fucking hope so," Arrow says before slapping me on the back.

I head to the gym we have set up in the clubhouse and do an hour of weights and boxing. I consider myself a good fighter, but not that I'd ever admit it out loud, it fucking hurts my ego that Decker, Cara's new man, is better than me. When I had gotten into trouble with the Forgotten Children, it was Decker who sort of saved the day. Fucker.

And he's obviously a good guy too, which is the only thing keeping me from going back after Cara and admitting the truth. She deserves better.

"You're back," Dice says as he steps into the gym, pulling his tank top off and getting onto the treadmill. I'm the one who brought Dice in after I almost got into a fight with him at a bar one day. Just as we were going to battle it out—over something I don't even remember—he said something that made me laugh instead. So I bought him a beer. He's had a hard life, but he's a good man to have at your back. He only just got patched in and I know he was meant for this life.

"Yep, what have I missed?" I ask.

"An epic ride," he calls out, starting to walk. "We rode all day yesterday. Prez had some business to take care of, and then we went to a bar."

"Sounds like a good day," I reply, low-key pissed I wasn't here. I love our group rides. I love being on my bike, period.

I need to sort my shit out. Drinking and fucking isn't going to get me anywhere.

"I saw Trisha. She asked where you were," he adds, referring to the woman Cara saw me kissing at Rift, a club the MC owns. It was the moment that sealed our breakup. The moment when I couldn't take back anything.

Trisha and I never slept together, although she has been trying for a while now. It was just that one kiss in front of Cara. And I know Trisha did nothing wrong, but I can imagine Cara's face falling if she ever saw Trisha and me together again. I would never do that to her. Besides, Trisha's not my type.

Dice laughs. "I'll tell her you've left the country next time."

"I'd appreciate that." I pause, and then say, "Learn from my lesson. Never fuck shit up with Leah." Leah is Dice's woman, and they have been together since high school. She's a beautiful Black woman, with long dark braids and a killer smile.

"I don't plan on it. I'm not an idiot."

Ouch.

"Good," I mutter under my breath. I wouldn't wish this shit on my worst enemy.

I finish my workout, have a long hot shower and then settle in my bedroom in the clubhouse, telling myself that I'm going to stay in tonight. I'm going to watch a movie, relax, and then tomorrow I'm going to get back to president-in-training shit.

I make it until eleven p.m. before I change my mind, get ready, throwing on my jeans and leather jacket, and rush out of there.

The last thing I want is to be left alone with my thoughts.

Chapter Five

Con
Two Months Later

Sitting at my desk, I glance around the Fast & Fury custom garage and smile. When Cara told me she'd managed to get me a job here, I was so nervous. I didn't know anything about motorcycles or design, and I didn't want to embarrass Cara if I wasn't good at the job. It would be her reputation on the line.

The two months I've been here, I have worked my ass off. I've come in early, I've stayed working late. I've researched motorcycles and seen all the work that gets done here, and I've watched, and I've listened.

I've learned so much in such a short time, and I actually love working here. The owner, Temper, is great, and the managers—twins by the name of Atlas and Aries—are total opposites. Atlas is funny and loud, and Aries is quiet, yet has a warm vibe about him. I feel comfortable going to any of them for help, depending on what I need help with. They're all members of the Knights of Fury MC, and I love all the staff. I actually look forward to my shifts, unlike at the bar, and

I'm respected here. They all listen to me when I speak, and are always checking in to make sure I'm okay. If I need a day off, I know that they will make that happen. It's a safe place to be.

I sent Cara a bunch of flowers to say thank you to her, but she played it off like it was nothing. To me, though, it was everything. No one does those kinds of things for me. She might be used to it, but I'm not.

And it makes me appreciate her even more.

"Good morning, Constance. We've got two people coming in to collect their new bikes today," Cam explains when she arrives. She's a blonde bombshell, tattooed and beautiful and extremely talented. Cam does all the artwork and designs on the motorcycles, while I run the merchandise shop and field any customer calls.

"Sounds good," I reply.

"Let me know if you need any help. I think this week we will show you how to check and order stock," she says, nodding thoughtfully. "You've been great to have here, you know that?"

I beam at the compliment. "Thank you, I'm loving being here."

"I hope you don't expect that enthusiasm from all of the staff here," Atlas says with a smirk as he joins us, glancing between the two of us. He's a good-looking man, and wherever he is, his twin isn't far away.

"Where's Aries?" Cam asks, as if reading my mind.

Atlas looks behind him to the entrance, just as Aries walks in. The two of them look so alike, only with minor differences, like Atlas has blue eyes while Aries has green.

"We'll go unload the stock," Atlas says, winking at me before heading to the storeroom.

"He's such a flirt," Cam mutters, shaking her head. She glances at her watch. "Okay, we're about to open. I'm going to go and make sure the bikes are flawless and ready for pickup."

"Of course they are flawless," I say as she walks away. She turns around and flashes me a grin. She's such a perfectionist, but that's probably why people pay so much for her custom designs. I assumed motor-cycles were expensive, especially the ones this garage does, but when I saw the first invoice my eyes shot out of my head. It was more expensive than a brand-new car and that was only half the bill.

The rest of the day goes quickly, and before I know it I'm in my car on my way home, which is about forty-five minutes away. It's a bit of a commute, but it's not too bad of a drive.

I bought myself this car after my last one was pushed off the road and damaged by some people who thought I was Cara. She and Decker tried to offer to buy me a new one, but my car was insured, so even though it wasn't worth much, I was still able to buy a new one. It's not fancy or anything, but it runs and it's good on gas, so I can't complain. It's better than the one I had before, so it's still an upgrade for me.

I park in my driveway, grab my beige handbag and get out of the car, looking up at my house. I still don't know if I made the right choice in taking over the mort-gage payments, because this house needs a lot of work and upkeep. I've been watching videos online and doing it all myself, but it's hard. I'm not very good at do-it-yourself projects, so it seems.

I step inside and lock the door behind me, heading straight for the kitchen and throwing my bag on the counter. I open the fridge and pull out some chocolate yogurt, and sit on the counter to eat it, sighing at the half-painted walls, the carpet that still needs removing and the hole in the wall I still haven't fixed, one that Dad made when he got angry and punched it.

My life is a mess.

I think that's why I like work so much. I just forget everything else and just focus on what I need to do. That way, it looks like I'm in control of my life, when clearly I'm just winging it and hoping for the best.

My phone chimes with a text from Cara.

Cara: How was work? Do you want to have dinner tonight?

Con: Yes, I'd love to. When and where?

Cara has been the light in my life, and I don't know if she realizes just how much. She's the only family I have left, the only family I would claim anyway, and I'm so glad that I found out about her. I know she has another sister, Natalie, but for me, she's all I've got. I don't speak to any of my other family, and haven't had any contact in some time.

Cara: My house. ASAP?

Con: Be there in twenty.

I put the yogurt I had planned on making my dinner back in the fridge, have a quick shower and get ready. I kind of feel like a fraud with Cara and her friends at times. They are all successful, wealthy and well-connected.

I wonder if they can tell that I'm the type of person who is always just hanging on by a thread.

When I pull up at Cara and Decker's house, I sigh when I see Clover's car there. Clover is an intimidating woman, and I know that she is skeptical of me. And I can see why. I'm Wade's daughter, which I know is a mark against me because Wade wasn't the best man, and I've only just come into the picture. Unlike Wade, though, I'd protect Cara at all costs, too, just like Clover. But I always feel like I'm trying to prove myself to her.

Cara greets me at the door with a smile, and I can hear music playing in the house. She's wearing a white T-shirt with jeans, her brown hair that matches mine dangling to her waist.

"Hey you, come on in," she says, opening the door wider. "Just letting you know that Decker is cooking tonight, so hopefully the food is edible."

I hide my smile and step inside. Clover is sitting on the couch with her daughter, Sapphire, on her lap, and Decker is sitting with Clover's husband, Felix, who is a police officer. Clover glances up and waves, but the energy I get from her isn't overly friendly. Ever since I've met her, Clover has always been pleasant, but I usually feel like the third wheel. I haven't been able to figure out how to crack her yet. Clover is a big part of Cara's life, and I'd like it if we could all be friends.

Clover has years of history with Cara, while all she and I share is blood.

"Hello," I say to all of them, waving and sitting down next to Felix. Much safer than sitting next to his wife.

"Hey, Con," Decker says warmly. "Can I get you something to drink? A glass of wine?"

"I'd love one."

He stands up and heads to the kitchen, returning with a glass of red.

"How was your day?" Cara asks, sitting down next to Clover, Sapphire jumping into her arms.

"It was good," I say. "I love working at the garage, and I'm learning so much. Most importantly, the people who work there are amazing."

"I'm glad." Cara nods, her eyes smiling at me.

"From what I've heard, they love you working there, too," Decker adds.

Decker is the private investigator I hired to find Cara for me. I guess in a way I brought the two of them together, which makes me think that all this was meant to be. He used to be partners with Felix on the police force and now works with Temper's sister-in-law. They are one of those big friendship groups where everyone knows everyone, and everyone dates everyone. I'd think it's weird if I weren't so jealous of the bonds they share.

I beam. "That's wonderful to know. I'm so much happier working there than at the bar."

"I better finish up dinner and get you all fed. Felix, you better come and supervise," Decker announces.

Felix laughs and follows him to the kitchen. "How times have changed."

"Yep, Felix cooks more than I do," Clover says, grinning.

"Hopefully he rubs off on Decker," Cara mutters, tucking her hair back behind her ear.

"Why does that sound dirty?" Clover replies, laughing. "And he's cooking tonight, so he's making an effort. What more can you ask for?"

"True. He is pretty wonderful." Cara sighs happily. "And he's not—"

"Bad to look at either," Clover finishes, and they both burst out laughing together.

The two of them are so close. I don't think I've ever met two women so in sync.

And yeah, I'm a little jealous.

"Well, to be honest, I threw him in the deep end tonight when I told him he's cooking," Cara admits, grinning.

"What is he cooking?" I ask, intrigued. Sapphire looks over at me with her gorgeous blue eyes, smiling widely. Her dark hair is tied up in a small ponytail on top of her head. Naturally, I smile back at her. She is so cute, maybe even the cutest child I've ever seen, and when she moves from Cara to come over to me, I let her sit on my lap. I can feel Clover's eyes on me, watching the interaction.

"Carbonara and garlic bread. Not too hard, so he can't mess it up. Aw, look, she likes you," Cara replies sweetly.

We hear loud banging noises coming from the kitchen. Clover's eyes head in that direction. "Well, worst-case, we can always order some pizza."

"Yeah, I have the pizza place on speed dial."

Sapphire touches my face and then moves off my lap, reaching for her mom to take her back. "She is so adorable," I tell Clover, who kisses her daughter and holds her.

"Thank you, we certainly think so."

"She doesn't usually like many people at first," Cara adds, sharing a look with Clover. "You must have a good aura about you, Con."

I decide to change the subject, not wanting to press my luck with Clover. "So I think I'm ready to start dating. Aside from the guy I had a one-night stand with a few months ago—"

"What guy?" Cara asks, giving me her attention.

"I met this really sexy guy at the bar, and I ended up going home with him," I admit.

Cara gasps. "No way! Good for you, about time you got some action! And are you going to see One-Night Stand Guy again?"

"You're already nicknaming him," Clover laughs.

"Just in case he becomes a thing," Cara says.

"Probably not." I shrug. "But I don't know, it's been so long since I've done anything like that."

"He must have been really hot then," Clover comments.

"He was," I reply, feeling my cheeks heat a little. "And extremely good in bed. I don't even know his name—"

"Oh, boy," Cara comments, grinning. "Why are you only mentioning this now? This is the stuff I need to hear."

"I don't know," I reply, shrugging. "I guess I feel a little more comfortable now and I don't think you would judge me."

"Of course not," Cara says, tone gentle. "We aren't prudes, you know. You can tell us anything."

"We aren't shy," Clover adds, grinning. "No detail is too small."

"Well," I state. "There was nothing small about this one."

We all start laughing.

"How's your new teaching job been going?" I ask Cara when the laughter subsides, as I sit cross-legged and sip the delicious wine.

"I'm loving it," she explains, lighting up. "The students are amazing, and the school has so much support."

"She's already making good changes at the school, too. Did you tell her about the breakfast club?" Clover asks.

Cara smiles and looks back at me. "I've started going in every morning and running a breakfast club, so the kids can all come in and eat before classes begin. Anyone is welcome, but of course the aim is to feed kids who might not otherwise have gotten anything to eat that morning."

"That's amazing, Cara. I wish I had that when I was growing up. I remember there were some mornings my mom and dad didn't bother to get up because they were hungover, and I had to sort myself out, pack my own lunch and get to school by myself. Having something like your program at my school would have been such a help."

Cara stills. "How old were you?"

"Five or so," I reply, looking down into my glass. I would have loved a hot breakfast, but instead I usually made myself cereal, sometimes without the milk if we didn't have any.

"I'm sorry, Con."

"Don't be sorry. I think it's so wonderful what you are doing for the kids who were like me, or have it even worse than I did."

"I hope I'm making a difference," Cara replies, nudging Clover gently. "And Clover donated money to help make it happen. So don't act like this was all me, Clo."

"It was all you. I just helped you fund it."

They both share a moment with each other, eyes connected. I know the two of them don't mean to make me feel like the third wheel, but I kind of do. To be fair, everyone probably feels that way when they are with these two. Even their partners.

We all have dinner, and Decker's carbonara surprises us all. Sapphire seeks me out again, sitting next to me and chatting away, telling little stories.

And then I head back home.

All alone.

Chapter Six

Rhett

"How's Clover?" I ask Sin as he grabs a beer out of the fridge and sits down next to me at the table.

Sin studies me and then just laughs. The asshole. "She's still pissed. What did you think would happen? You know that she likes to hold on to a grudge. You cheated on Cara, broke up your little best friend trio and showed her that some men ain't shit. Men she thought were good men."

"I'm still a good man," I grumble, scrubbing my hand down my jaw. "But I'm not fucking perfect. What do you think I should do?"

"I think that your apology has to be as big as your fuckup," he says, slapping me on the shoulder. "So you better make it a good one."

Cara forgave me faster than Clover did, and she's the one who thinks I cheated on her.

Typical fucking Clover.

"She really showed who her favorite best friend was, didn't she?" I mutter, just as Rake steps into the clubhouse kitchen and eyes Sin and me sitting around having a drink. "So much for loving us all the same."

I sound like a kid, I know, but I've been friends with these girls since I was a damn kid, so it's easy to go back there.

"Girls still not talking to you?" Rake asks, sitting down and joining us for a beer. I know he was disappointed in the fact that I hurt his daughter, but apparently Cara is *so* happy and well loved now that everyone can see that this all happened for a reason. Except Clover.

And yeah, that hurts like a kick straight to my nuts, because now it's making me question everything. Was I loving Cara wrong the entire time we were together?

Maybe I'm broken. Maybe I'm meant to be the single man-whore for the rest of my time. I mean, it doesn't sound so bad. I could focus on the club and dedicate my life to the Wind Dragons without anyone holding me back, which I guess was the original plan.

I'd say without having any weaknesses, but together or not, Cara will always be a weakness of mine. And Clover. Those two need me and I'd be there in a second.

I'd shoot first and ask questions later.

I'd start a war for either of them.

"They are, but it's just not the same. I don't know if it ever will be, to be honest," I admit.

Rake flips the bottle cap off his beer and takes a swig. "You going to give up that easily?"

I mean, my ego is hurt.

My heart, also hurt.

My dick—that one feels great, but then makes me feel guilty, so also not my friend right now.

And then the fact that I've lied to not only Cara by letting her think I betrayed her, but my whole family too, doesn't sit right with me either. More guilt.

What have I got left?

The Wind Dragons.

They better fucking be worth it.

When I take over as president there will be some changes, and I hope I'm not met with any resistance. Arrow has been running the show here for a long time, and when I take over, being much younger and inexperienced, I know that some of the members are going to test me along the way to see if I'm strong enough to lead them. They need to trust me and my judgment or they won't want me leading the MC.

And I need to be ready for that. A club is only as strong as its president.

"No, but I think I'm going to give them a little more time before I show up with a boom box outside their windows."

The men laugh. "Now that, I'd like to see," Sin mutters.

"Bet he gets shot," Rake adds, his cheerful tone making me wonder if he'd low-key like that to happen.

Arrow steps into the kitchen, his eyes going straight to me. "We have some business, if you guys are done fucking around."

He steps back out, and just like that we all stand in unison and follow our president.

I make the two-hour drive and deliver the package as Arrow requested, which was the business in question. After that, I head out to get some food. Finding myself in my regular watering hole, I've sat down and ordered something to eat and a beer when I notice a familiar face sitting alone at the bar.

I walk over to her, her vanilla scent hitting me before she even notices me. "Hello."

"Hey." She smiles, glancing up in surprise. Most people seem to rave on about blue or light-colored eyes, but when those brown eyes look at me, I suddenly feel weak in the knees. Nothing is as beautiful. "Fancy seeing you here."

"We must be creatures of habit." I grin, sitting down next to her.

She smirks back, resting her chin on her palm, her dark hair a curtain around her pretty face. She looks fucking cute, wearing a denim dress and red lipstick.

"You here alone?" I ask.

"Yeah," she replies. "I am now. My friend Jamie left, so I was just about to get out of here."

"And now that I'm here?"

"And now…" She bites her bottom lip seductively. "I'm still about to go home."

I laugh out loud. She has fire, and I like that. "Ahh, come on now. Have a drink. Or some of my chicken wings when they arrive."

She pauses and tilts her head to the side. "I suppose I could stay for a chicken wing. And for some company. Going home to an empty house every night is getting a little old. It's so…quiet."

I scan her eyes, surprised by her vulnerability. "I know what you mean. I try to stay home, but it never happens. I always need the distraction." I've never admitted that out loud to anyone.

Our eyes connect and hold. "Well, I'm glad we ran into each other then."

"Me too," I say softly.

"So I'm embarrassed to ask this, but what is your name?"

I laugh, realizing that we may have swapped bodily fluids but have yet to formally introduce ourselves. I reach my hand out for her to shake. "I'm Rhett."

She smiles and places her delicate, warm hand in mine, giving it a squeeze. "Constance, but people call me Con."

"Not Connie?" I ask, teasing her.

She makes a face. "No, please never Connie."

I order her a drink, and then we get talking, and I find out we actually have a fair bit in common. We like the same kind of music and bands, and she's into outdoorsy shit like camping, four-wheel driving and fishing, which does surprise me. She also seems to have a girlie side, so she is quite the walking contradiction. She appears to know how to have a good time out of the bedroom too, which is really cool. I've never met a woman who has so many similar interests to me, including Cara.

"I can't believe you play the guitar, too," I say, studying her.

"I haven't played in a few months, to be honest," she says. "Have you ever been to the open mic nights here? Some really cool bands come and play. I think you'd really like them."

"I haven't, but I'd like to. Can you sing, too?"

"A little," she replies, looking down shyly.

"I'd love to hear that," I say quietly.

"Maybe one day," she replies. "When is the last time you went camping?"

"It's been a while actually," I admit, realizing that I haven't really been doing much outside of the club. "I was supposed to do a beach trip with my friends recently, but I had to cancel because I've been so busy. How about you?"

"I went camping by myself a couple of months ago. Off the grid, no internet."

"That sounds pretty amazing, like a reset."

She nods. "It was."

"I don't know any woman who would do something like that by themselves. In a group, yes, but not alone."

"I don't mind my own company, but it does get a little boring," she says. She's so strong and independent, and I hope that she knows that.

The food arrives, and Con licking all the sauce off her fingers is all the foreplay I'm going to need tonight.

We finish our drinks, the conversation flowing. I realize that I really like spending time with her and I've enjoyed her company tonight. I pay the bill and we stand and leave.

"I'll walk you to your car," I say, and fall into step with her.

She clears her throat. I know what she's thinking, because I'm thinking the same thing. I don't want the night to end just yet, but getting to know her more personally is also making me feel like this is getting a little more complicated than just a hookup, and I don't know how I feel about that.

I don't want her to get hurt, and right now I'm a fucking mess. I need something simple and easy. At the same time, I do like her, and we are very compatible in the sheets.

"Do you want to come over for some coffee?" she asks, leaning against the open car door. "I mean, only if you want to, of course."

I smile at her attempt to be bold, but her nervous energy seeps in. She's fucking adorable. But I don't know if it's a good idea to sleep with the same woman more than once. I've kept my hookups one and done. It will be crossing into new territory for me, and I don't know if I'm ready for that. But I genuinely like her.

"Okay, sure. I'll follow you."

I get in my car and park behind hers when we arrive at her house. She unlocks the door while I get out and waits for me at the front. I want to push her back against the door and pin her arms up against the wood and kiss her like we did last time, but I don't. Hell, maybe she really just wants me over for some coffee, and coming to her house for the second time is a hell of a lot different than the first time. One, we're both sober, and two, I know her a little more now.

She's not just a pretty face and a hot body.

As we step inside I notice she's been renovating her house. There's a half-painted wall waiting to be finished and tools lying about the place.

"Sorry about the mess," she apologizes. "Hopefully I'll be done with this wall this week."

"You're doing all of it by yourself?" I ask, impressed.

She nods. "Yeah, it's taken me longer, but I'm slowly getting there. This is how I've been spending all my days off." She steps closer to me, her eyes landing on my lips. "So, uhh, did you want some…coffee?"

I grin and tuck her hair back behind her ear. "Sure."

I'm about to lean in to kiss her when she heads into the kitchen...and actually starts making me some coffee.

"So coffee wasn't a euphemism for sex?" I ask, confused. She puts the kettle down and turns around, trying to keep a straight face. "I mean, I'm happy to have some coffee, if that's all your offering, I just thought..."

She starts to laugh. "Yeah, I just didn't know... I don't know what we are doing here."

"I don't know either," I admit quietly.

She looks down at the mug and then back at me. "So do you want coffee?"

I laugh, and she comes over to me until our bodies are touching, and all the laughter disappears. "We don't have to overthink it, right?"

She nods. "It's just casual."

We stare at each other until suddenly we're heatedly kissing. We're both panting when we pull apart, and she nods to her bedroom. "Follow me."

She turns to lead the way, and I stand behind her and push all her hair to her left shoulder, my fingers brushing against her skin. She leans against me, rests her head back and closes her eyes. She's obviously a very independent woman, and I can respect that. But the way she melts against me lets me know she's ready for me to take a little control, and allow her to just relax.

I kiss the side of her neck, and a little gasp falls from her lips. I then spin her around and kiss her again, gentle at first and then deeper. I slowly walk her backward to her bedroom and turn the light on, then lay her down on the bed, stripping off her clothes and taking my time with her. I enjoy the view of the beautiful bare body, nothing on her now except red lipstick, and I can't wait to see those red lips wrapped around my cock. I stand back and undress myself, her eyes on me, sexy as fuck, especially when her gaze drops.

I'm hard. Fuck, I've been hard since I saw her sitting at the bar.

I straddle her, careful not to put all my weight on her, and kiss my way down her body.

This experience is different for me.

This is the first time I've slept with someone sober since Cara.

I know how bad that sounds, but I've been mostly picking up women after I've had a few drinks, and if I'm being honest, I've been drunk most of the time ever since I became single, including the night Con and I had a few months ago.

Con is the first woman I'm giving myself to with a clear mind.

I wonder if she knows how big that is for me.

She threads her fingers through my hair and tugs gently, encouraging me as I start to lick her pussy.

I give her a devilish smile and forget everything else; my mind is consumed by Con, by her body, and by just wanting to please her.

After she comes, she kneels before me on the carpet. I see those red lips where I want them, and it's a better sight than I even imagined.

Yeah, life isn't as bad as I've been making it out to be.

Chapter Seven

Con

I don't know what it is about Rhett.

Yeah, he's possibly the hottest guy I've ever seen in real life, and yeah, he's fucking amazing in bed and obviously well experienced. But it's something a little deeper than that.

When I look into his eyes, I see the same thing that I see in my own in the mirror.

Loneliness.

He's seeking a connection, even if it's just for a night or two.

I know how he feels.

Before he leaves my house the next morning, he asks me for my phone and programs his number into it, sending a text to himself so now we have a way to contact one another.

He flashes me a smile before he leaves, and I sag against my front door after I close and lock it. Last night was different than the first time we slept together. He left the light on, so there was nothing we didn't see. There was eye contact, and I don't know...

There was a connection there.

And neither of us was drunk.

I don't want to read too much into it, because for all I know he might do a runner now and never text me at all, but yeah.

I want to see him again.

And I know it's probably not the best idea, because someone is going to get hurt, most likely me if I start having feelings for him, but I like him, and I'm admitting that to myself.

The sex was bomb, and even better than last time. The man is talented with his tongue, fingers and cock. Talk about a trifecta.

I have a long bath, pampering myself a little with candles, music and a bath bomb, and then once I'm dressed, I pick up my guitar for the first time in months and play.

The truth is, I haven't felt this good in a long time.

And I don't want that to go away.

I see him again a few times during the week and that next weekend.

"So I know this isn't a romantic idea," he says after showing up at my house on a Saturday morning, grinning, leaning his forearm against my door. "But I came to finish shit in your house for you. I've been told I'm pretty handy."

"Oh, you're handy all right, but you don't need to help me do anything, Rhett. That's my problem, not yours."

Although the thought is so fucking sweet. So sweet I don't even know how to react. I thought he was back for only more sex, but he's offering to paint the walls for me. I don't know what to say.

He ignores my comment. "Put me to work, Con. You shouldn't be doing all of this stuff by yourself. It will be faster if there's two of us."

I blink quickly so he can't see the tears in my eyes. No one has offered their help to me so easily. No one except Cara.

Is this what it feels like being able to rely on someone?

"Okay," I whisper, clearing my throat.

He lifts my chin up with his fingers, scans my eyes and kisses me. "And then maybe I could take you out for dinner? A real dinner this time."

I swallow hard, wanting to pinch myself. Is this man for real?

"Okay," I manage to say again.

He leaves me standing there, blown away, and starts prepping everything to finish painting the wall. Eventually, when I accept the situation, I join him and start to help. We put some music on, and let me tell you, it's a million times more fun having someone with you when doing stuff around the house. A million.

Plus, he's much taller than me, and he doesn't even need to use the ladder.

"You didn't have to come and help me, but I appreciate it," I say, smiling and letting out a sigh at the same time. "You surprised me. I didn't know there were good men like you left in the world."

"I'm not as good as you might think," he mutters. "But I'm happy to help. You shouldn't have to do all this by yourself."

I get us some soda out of the fridge and the two of us paint alongside each other, working as a team. And a pretty good one at that.

After we're finished with the wall, we clean up, take a shower together and go out for dinner, where I insist on paying, and afterward Rhett stays the night. I don't know what's happening here exactly, but it's exciting.

He makes me feel alive.

Connected.

Human.

"Good night," he whispers, kissing my neck.

The next morning he's gone before I wake up.

And I can't stop smiling for the rest of the day.

Monday comes around and I'm back at work. Rhett has been texting me, and it's been nice getting to know him that way, too.

"You look…different," Cam says as she studies me. "You're glowing. Either you got laid, or you are pregnant."

"I'm definitely not pregnant," I comment back, laughing.

Cam grins widely. "Good for you."

"What's good for her?" Atlas interrupts, being nosy.

"Nothing," Cam says to him, rolling her eyes. "Woman talk."

Atlas arches his brow. "I'm not a boy, Cam. I'm a man. That shit doesn't faze me. You on your period? Need me to go to the store? I can buy tampons, pads. Just let me know what pussy size you are."

"Thank you, Atlas," I say through uncontrollable

laughter. "I'm not on my period, but you'll be the first to know when I am."

Aries walks over to his brother and whispers something into his ear. Atlas nods, then turns back to us. "Temper needs us. Can you hold down the fort while I go and see what's up?"

Cam checks the daily schedule. "Yeah, we should be able to manage without you. Go see what the boss needs."

We watch them leave, and I have to wonder what kind of stuff Temper needs them to do. I want to ask, but I don't. I've only just started here and the last thing I want is them to think I'm being nosy about their business. I'm aware that they're in an MC, but I really don't know what that involves.

"Victoria will be in soon, so I'll have you two out the front and I'll be out the back. Call me if you need help with anything." Victoria is our part-time receptionist, but like me, she's an all-rounder and helps with whatever we need. There's also Bronte, who works here doing all the back-end administrative stuff, but today is her day off. Along with Atlas, Aries and Diesel, another member of the Knights of Fury, that makes up our team. Cam said that she's looking at hiring another mechanic, but she hasn't found anyone who fits her criteria just yet.

I sent Rhett a text this morning asking him what his plans are this weekend.

Rhett: I'm busy this weekend, sorry.

Con: Okay, no worries. Rain check.

Rhett: Definitely.

While I'm disappointed, I'm beginning to like this casual thing we have going. There are no real expectations and no hurt feelings. We see each other whenever we can, and I really enjoy the time we spend together. Quality over quantity.

I spend my morning restocking the merchandise shelves, putting prices on things and helping customers who walk in.

I can't help feel like ever since Cara came into my life I've been on a run of good luck. New job, new car, and now a new man has entered my life. One that fate seems to keep putting in front of me, first at the bar, then twice more. The fourth time he brought himself back to my house. I know he's a biker, but he hasn't spoken about that part of his life, and I haven't asked. I figure he will tell me what he wants me to know. I considered asking someone at work if they know him and what his deal is, but I decided not to. He will tell me when he's ready. He hasn't worn his leather cut around me since I first saw him in it in the bar, so I'm not sure if that's a coincidence or on purpose.

I'm not sure about a lot of things.

Maybe I'll ask Cara and Clover if they would like to go shopping with me this weekend instead. Or we could go out for lunch or something. Ever since I started working here, I've been making a lot more money than at my old job, so it's been nice to have a little extra money after each payday. I'm still living paycheck to paycheck, but it's nowhere near as bad anymore, and I've slowly been paying off my debts. I even read a few books on finance, because I know I needed help to sort mine out. Give me a few years and I'll be back on top of life, debt free and with a huge savings account.

It feels good to be able to look forward to the future.

And I didn't even have to become a stripper, like my mom was and like I thought I'd eventually be when I became desperate for more money. Maybe eventually I could even go back to college, part-time even, and work on getting my degree.

I have so many opportunities now, and maybe all I needed was a little push, and to believe in myself.

And now it's all coming together.

Chapter Eight

Rhett

"Who are you texting so much?" Dice asks me, nosily trying to look at my phone screen. We're all at the clubhouse, hanging out.

"A friend," I say, closing down my app so he can't see. "You nosy fucker."

"Just one? Not plural? That doesn't sound like you," he comments, the smart-ass.

Sledge, another prospect who just got patched in, smirks. "When you find the golden pussy, you don't need plural."

I'm about to knock these two out. Although with Sledge, I'm glad he's on our side. He's well over six feet tall and built like a brick house; he's easily the biggest man we have in the MC.

None of them have met Con yet, and I don't know when that will happen. I felt bad telling her that I'm busy this weekend when the truth is, I wish I could take her with me to the party I'm going to. I'm not looking forward to it at all, but I know that I have to go. It would be nice to have someone on my side, someone to help me navigate the night, but I don't want to put her in that position. Although having her there might alleviate some of the tension between me and Cara.

But with everyone thinking that I'm a cheat—including my mom, who heard it from the grapevine—and Cara and Clover there, I don't know if it's a smart move.

I'm torn. I could just tell them all that Con is a friend of mine, and maybe it won't be a big deal at all.

I don't know.

I don't want to throw Con into the deep end that is my family drama, but I also do want her to be there. But then if I invite her, am I taking this from casual to serious?

Fuck.

Cara is happily in a new relationship with a man she lives with, so why do I have to walk on eggshells?

Maybe I should just bring Con and let her meet everyone. While I don't know what exactly this is, I know I enjoy her company and more than just in bed.

Rhett: I know I said I was busy this weekend, but the truth is, I have a party I have to go to. Do you want to come with me?

Con: I'd love to.

Shit. I guess I'm doing this.

Rhett: I can come and pick you up?

Con: No, it's okay. I can drive there.

I have to try to explain the situation to her; I don't want her walking in there blind. But how does one explain this shit show without scaring her away?

Rhett: I should probably tell you that my ex will be there with her new partner.

Con: Okay. That's nice, that you guys can all be friends. Thanks for the heads up.

Shit. I want to explain to her that we aren't exactly on great terms, but I decide to leave it. It might be perfectly fine after all. Who am I kidding? It will be a shit show.

And now when the MC sees Con, they will know that she's the one I've been texting so much.

"We going for a ride or what?" I ask, sliding my phone away. Dice and Sledge instantly stop messing around and we get on our bikes.

The truth is, I'm not sure how this party is going to go. I probably should explain the situation to her in more detail, but I honestly don't know how. I don't want to lie to her like I'm lying to everyone else.

By the way, it's a biker party for my ex's sister, so my ex and her family will also be there, and they don't know I'm seeing anyone and think I'm a huge cheater because I let them think that, so it might be awkward. But I want you there with me.

Yeah, I'm a selfish fuck, but it's true.

I want her there.

We've been texting, calling and seeing each other ever since we exchanged numbers, and she's become a big part of my life really quickly. I don't know how she got my guard down, and I have no idea how this all happened.

For the first time in a long time, I feel good. I'm smiling at my phone like a fucking idiot, I'm not drinking just to get through the night, and I don't feel so alone in the world. Con is sweet, she's rough around the edges in a way that attracts me to her, and she's down-to-earth and real. And she's beautiful. She smells like vanilla and she's funny.

And maybe Cara and Clover will like her.

Then with their blessing maybe I can finally move on. Maybe Con is the person I'm supposed to be with and I can pursue a romantic relationship with her. This is what everyone has been telling me, that there is someone else out there for me. I mean, I want to take it slow with her, but this can be a first step.

I guess we will just have to see how this plays out.

And if it's meant to be, it will be.

The weekend rolls around quickly. I didn't want Con to meet me at the clubhouse and have to walk in alone, so I told her to meet me at my house. Mine and Cara's house. I know it's fucked-up, but I had nowhere else to tell her to meet me. So now I'm standing out the front of my old house that I used to live in with my ex and waiting to take this new girl to a club party.

Why did I think this was a good idea again? I offered to pick Con up because I felt bad that she had to do the long drive for me. I'm used to it, but she won't be, and her car doesn't look as reliable as I'd like. But she insisted that she doesn't mind driving up by herself.

Like I said, independent.

She pulls up in her little red car and I smile when I lay eyes on her. When she parks I walk over and open the car door for her, pulling her into my arms and giving her a warm hug. "You made it."

"I did." She looks beautiful, in tight black belted jeans, boots and one of those tops that shows a little of her stomach. Her hair and makeup are done, and she just looks effortlessly sexy.

"You look…"

"Tired?"

"Perfect."

She smiles and lets out a small sigh, like she is relieved. "So this is your house?" she asks, taking in the vast open gates. "Is this a bad neighborhood or are you just big on security?"

I smirk. "It's technically my house."

She arches her brow. "What does that mean?"

I wrap my arm around her. "It is mine, but I'm selling it, so I'm not actually staying here right now." I decide to quickly change the subject, not wanting to get into that. "You ever been on the back of a motorcycle?"

She shakes her head, and the pleasure her reply gives me, only a possessive biker would understand.

"I thought we could take the bike," I explain.

She touches her hair, but then shrugs. "Okay, sounds good to me."

She locks her car, and I put my spare helmet on her, then kiss her. When she opens her eyes, she smiles at me. "You know, you never even told me whose party we are going to."

Oh, I know.

"A friend of mine. Her name is Natty," I explain.

"I've known her and her family for years now. I should also probably tell you that the party is at a biker club-house. Don't worry, it's safe, and it's a family party."

"Okay." She nods. "Did we bring Natty a present?"

I grin. "We did. I got her a gold necklace with an evil eye pendant on it. I gave it to her early." I dropped it off at her front door because she's still pissed at me too, but Con doesn't need to know that.

Why am I going again? Oh, right, because even if they are holding a grudge against me or not, they are still my family, and I'm theirs.

Whether they like it or not.

I lift Con up onto the back of my bike, my hands on her hips. She straddles it and smiles over at me, excitement in her eyes. I show her where to put her feet, and then climb on in front of her.

"Hold on to me and just enjoy the ride," I say, bringing her arms around me.

She scoots forward and rests her body against my back, gripping on to me for dear life, and it feels so good to have her there. No one has been on the back of my bike except Cara and Clover, and Clover was only on there because Cara let her. Con might not know it, but it's a big deal for me.

And everyone that sees us showing up like this will know that it is, too.

So I guess tonight is more than just a shit show—I'm also showing my club that Con does mean something to me.

How they'll take it is another thing.

We ride to the clubhouse, and I purposely take the longer route so we can have a lengthier ride together.

Her grip lessens, so I know she's more comfortable and hopefully enjoying herself. If she hated riding, it would be pretty fucking difficult.

The clubhouse is packed when we get there, loud music, cars and motorcycles parked everywhere. I park in the corner and help Con get off the bike.

"What did you think?" I ask, helping her take her helmet off.

"I loved it," she says, smiling as she attempts to fix her hair. "I want to ride one. I mean, I work with bikes all day in the garage; I might as well learn to ride. Could you teach me?"

Fuck.

I get hard at the thought of her riding.

When she told me she had started work at a bike garage, I have to admit I was surprised and impressed. And then when she mentioned it was Fast & Fury, it kind of seemed too good to be true. I think the Knights of Fury own that garage, so it's a bit of a small world. They helped me out of a jam when I got into some trouble months ago. Normally MCs keep to themselves, but I owe them one, even if they have a connection to Decker. Con is obviously comfortable around bikers, and maybe she would like the lifestyle that comes with being with one?

Swallowing hard, I nod. "Yeah, I think I could."

"Sweet," she replies, glancing toward the clubhouse. "Anything I should know or expect before I walk in there?"

I wince, and she doesn't miss it. "What?" she asks, brow furrowing.

I wrap my arm around her. "Well, my mom and dad

will be here, so I probably should have warned you about that."

"Really?" she asks as I lead her to the entrance.

"Yeah, and the rest of my family." I leave it at that, because any more and she will probably not walk through that threshold.

To be fair, tonight could go fine, without any hiccups. I told her that my ex is going to be here, so it could get a little awkward, but Cara isn't a mean person, so Con has nothing to worry about.

So then why am I sweating?

Chapter Nine

Con

Rhett takes my hand in his, which makes me feel super comfortable and proud to arrive with him. I thought it was incredibly sweet when Rhett offered to do the drive to come and pick me up. I have to question if all men are like that, or have I just been previously dating the scum of the earth? I don't know any men who would drive two hours to pick me up, then two hours back, just so I didn't have to drive if I didn't want to.

As we walk through the clubhouse, I take it all in, looking around and being quite surprised. The place is beautiful, spacious, modern, and looks to be newly renovated. They obviously love the finer things in life, like leather and muted colors.

When Rhett invited me to this party, I have to admit that I had a few questions. Like why didn't he initially invite me? Maybe he was wondering if it was the right time to meet his family, which I understand. We aren't even an official couple, so it's all very new.

Or maybe he's just going to introduce me as a friend,

which I'm also okay with, because technically that's all I am.

Okay, I need to stop overthinking this, and just let myself enjoy the time with him. The key to happiness is having low, or no, expectations, and I need to re-member that. I just want to meet his people and find out more about him in this setting, which I am excited for. I made sure to look my best to make a good impression.

"This isn't what I thought a biker clubhouse would look like," I admit, eyes on the expensive-looking paint-ings hanging on the white walls.

Rhett laughs and gives my fingers a gentle squeeze. "Yeah, we get that a lot. It's been done up over the years, and everything was slowly replaced and upgraded." He points to a wall that is covered from top to bottom in mug shots. "See, I'm not on there. I'm a good boy."

I can't believe they have so many mug shots, but hey, what did I expect coming into a biker clubhouse? I shake my head at him, hiding my smile. "Never say never."

Rhett laughs, his beautiful blue eyes crinkling at the corners. "You know what? I think you'll fit in fine here."

That makes me relax even more.

Maybe these are my people, the ones who won't judge my mother for having been a stripper, for my dad being a little shady of character and for me not being the perfect woman the world expects me to be.

I recognize the redheaded man from the restaurant when I first met Rhett as he approaches us. "Con, this is Dice. Dice, Con."

He offers me his hand and I take it. "Nice to meet you."

"You too," I say, smiling at him.

"So you finally texted him back," he teases, remembering when Rhett handed me his number that night.

"Something like that."

He shares a look with Rhett and nods. In approval? I don't know. "Birthday girl is out the back."

"Thanks, brother."

Rhett leads me through a bunch of people, all of whom he says hello to, and all of whom stare at me curiously. When we get past them, he opens the sliding door for me, still holding my hand, and I step outside to about twenty people, all of them surrounding a large, amazing-looking platter of food.

We take a few steps toward the group and I notice that everyone is staring at us.

Everyone.

I don't know if it's me squeezing the shit out of Rhett's hand, or him with mine, but our grips are tight and unmoving.

A woman appears from the crowd, and I relax and smile when I recognize her. What is my sister doing at this biker party? I mean, I know she grew up with bikers of course, but I still wasn't expecting to see her tonight.

Cara steps forward, but instead of her smiling and excited to see me, she looks confused and surprised.

Maybe even a little...hurt?

"Cara?" I call out in question, and Rhett's head snaps to me instantly.

"You know her?" he asks. I frown at his harsh tone.

Clover appears next to Cara, and the two of them approach us.

"Cara," I say, glad I'm going to have someone to hang out with while here.

"You're kidding me, right, Rhett?" Cara whispers, eyes filling with hurt.

Clover's eyes are pinned on me, filled with anger. I take a step back. "Nice to see you showing your true colors, Con."

I'm confused. They both look so mad, and I don't know what we've done wrong. I never want to see Cara upset, and I just want to fix whatever is wrong.

"What's going on? Cara, I didn't know you'd be here," I say, but Cara refuses to look at me.

Another girl comes and joins us. She has beautiful green eyes, done with cat eyeliner, and long dark hair. She's wearing a birthday sash, which lets me know that she is Natty, the birthday girl.

It's then that a feeling of dread comes over me. Natty. Natalie. Cara's sister is Natalie.

"What is going on here?" she asks, glancing between Rhett and I. "Who is this?"

"This is Con," Clover informs Natty. "And she's here *with* Rhett."

Natty's eyes widen, and her mouth drops a little. "Con? As in…?"

"Yep," Clover says.

"What the fuck is going on here?" Rhett asks Cara, letting go of my hand, and I feel the absence immediately. "Cara?"

Cara looks between us and then just walks away, disappearing inside. Clover and Natty watch her leave, and then turn their fury onto us.

"I knew you wanted to be part of her life, but never once did I think you'd pull something like this," Clover says, shaking her head. She could have slapped me across the face because her words feel that way.

She looks up at Rhett. "And you. I'm so angry right now I can't even be around you. You have no shame. You're so much better than this, Rhett." She storms off after her best friend.

Natty crosses her arms and purses her lips together before speaking. "I don't even know what to say right now." She turns to me. "And Cara spoke so highly of you, Con."

"Natty—" Rhett grits out between clenched teeth.

She turns to Rhett and cuts him off straightaway. "And you. Can't have Cara back so you go for the *Wish* version? Desperate even for you."

Ouch.

And that's when I finally understand just how much I have messed up.

Rhett is Cara's ex-boyfriend.

Natty is her sister.

And this clubhouse I've just walked into?

It's her home.

I turn around and get the hell out of there.

I retrace my steps until I'm outside and standing next to Rhett's bike. I don't know how I'm going to get back to my car, but I need to leave right now. I've never been more humiliated in my life.

I can't believe that Rhett is Cara's ex-boyfriend. I truly had no idea, since she has never spoken about anyone to me except Decker. She did mention an ex, but she never told me his name. I hope she believes me when I say that I never would have slept with him, or given him a second of my time, if I knew who he was.

I have the worst luck.

"What the fuck was that in there?" Rhett asks me as he walks over. He looks angry, and I don't know how I'm suddenly the bad person in all of this. "How do you know Cara and Clover? What were they talking about?"

"Cara is my sister."

His eyes widen and he stares at me as if he has never seen me before. Like he didn't lie in bed for hours with me.

"Half sister, actually," I say in defeat. Saying it out loud makes this all more real.

"I heard Wade had another kid, but I didn't know you had connections with her."

"Surprise!" I say, sarcasm dripping.

"Did you know?"

"Know what?"

"That Cara was my ex?"

"No! Of course I didn't know. I'd never want to hurt Cara," I reply, beginning to pace. "How did *you* not know?"

"I'm not exactly in the know with Cara's life anymore. You came into Cara's life at a time where she and I...well, it was toward the end of our relationship," he explains, gritting his teeth together. "What a fucking mess."

"You're telling me. She's going to hate me now, and Clover already hated me, so now she actually has a reason," I say, taking a few deep breaths to calm myself down. "I didn't want to give her a reason," I whisper, tears on the verge of falling. "I need to get back to my car. I need to leave."

"You're not driving home two hours when you're

upset," he says, scrubbing his hand down his face. "Come on, let's get out of here before Rake finds me."

I don't know who Rake is, but I'd do anything to leave, so I jump on the back of his bike and we ride out of there. This ride is completely different to the one on the way here. I don't lean into him, and I don't smile. I don't enjoy myself. I just think about the look of betrayal on Cara's face.

She's never going to trust me now, and she's not going to want me in her life.

What Clover and Cara's sister said? That hurt.

I just want to go home and cry and figure out how I can make this up to Cara.

And I can never see Rhett again.

The ride goes on for what feels like double the amount of time it took to arrive, and I know it's because every second on here feels like a minute. Or an hour.

When we finally pull up to his house, I get off the second the bike comes to a stop and wait for him to open the gates. I then walk over to my car. This date has to be one of the worst nights of my life. What a waste of my time. I should have just stayed single like I usually do, and ignored any men who look my way. Yes, I'm being melodramatic, but I just potentially lost my sister. Again.

"Where are you going? You can't just drive home like this," he says, moving in front of me and blocking my access to the driver's door.

"What do you expect me to do? Just stay at your house and pretend this never happened? That the sister I only just found doesn't hate me?" I ask, crossing my arms over my chest. "That was all of her family there, and that is the first impression I made. Imagine what everyone thinks of me!"

"Con, we didn't know," he says calmly, eyes scanning mine. "We aren't bad people. I didn't know you were her sister, and you didn't know I was her ex. We have nothing to feel guilty about."

"They don't know that, though."

"They will when I get to explain our side of the story," he says, sighing. "I'm sorry the night turned out like this. I invited you because I wanted you there while I saw Clover and Cara for the first time in a while. Do you know the history we have?"

I shake my head. Oh great, did Rhett date Clover, too?

"Will you at least come in so I can explain what happened? If you want to leave and never talk to me again, I'll understand."

I contemplate my options, but my curiosity gets the best of me. "Okay, but I'm not staying." He nods.

I follow him inside and the first thing I see are pictures of him and Cara decorating the walls.

"You've got to be fucking kidding me!" I say, and move to leave.

Rhett whips his head to see what sparked the reaction out of me and winces. "Con, wait, no. I haven't stayed in this house since Cara left. I only asked you to meet me here 'cause I don't have another place. I promise I have not been living here."

I give him a short nod. "Why don't you just tell me the CliffsNotes version of what happened?"

Rhett moves to sit on the couch, lets out a loud breath and tells me the whole tragic story of Cara and him and the history he shares with her and Clover. After he finishes, I'm quiet for a long time.

"That is a lot to process. Thank you for telling me that; I'm sure it wasn't easy."

"I'm sorry that Clover and Natty said those things to you. None of that is true. Why don't you let me book you a hotel if you don't want to stay with me? I don't want you driving two hours in the dark while you're upset."

I reluctantly agree. "Okay, I'll stay in a hotel and drive home tomorrow."

Going straight to bed sounds wonderful. Even though I didn't plan on spending the night alone. I guess it will just be me and my guilty conscience for the night.

Tonight with Rhett was one huge red flag.

Worst date ever.

Chapter Ten

Rhett

Tonight couldn't have gone worse if I'd tried. All the people I care about are hurt right now, and I don't know how to fix it.

Con didn't say much after I told her the abridged version of everything—although I didn't tell her about everyone thinking I'm a cheater. She doesn't need to know that. I dropped her off at the best hotel in town and paid for a night's stay, and she left for her room before I could even say goodbye. She doesn't want anything to do with me, and I know it's because she's hurt, and humiliated, but none of this was intentional. I don't know how I can make it up to her.

And then there is Cara. The look on her face... I'd take Clover's and Natty's anger over that any day.

I cannot believe the odds. I fell for Cara's half sister. Of all the women in the world, she is the one I wanted to start building a relationship with. I've destroyed so much with one selfish choice—my relationship with Con, Con and Cara's relationship, my friendship with Clover. The list goes on.

I sit back in my old leather chair and finish the last of my scotch. I didn't want to go back to the clubhouse so now I'm sitting at my old house, filled with memories of me and Cara, drowning my sorrows and thinking about Con.

I like her. And yeah, I guess now that I think about it at the start she kind of did remind me of Cara in her looks a little, but she's nothing like Cara. The reasons why I like her have nothing to do with Cara. This whole thing is so fucked-up, and I don't know where to begin with trying to fix it. I decide to send everyone a text, starting with Con.

To Con: I'm so sorry about tonight. Can we please talk tomorrow?

To Cara: I had no idea she was your sister, and she had no idea I was your ex. We are so sorry.

I want to add that we did nothing wrong because we didn't know, but decide not to.

To Clover: I had no idea she was Cara's sister. You two have told me nothing recently! I'm sorry.

To Natty: I had no idea. I'm sorry for causing drama at your birthday.

Who else do I owe an apology to? The list is long. I text my mom and say I'm sorry for leaving without seeing her, and for what happened. She's no doubt going to have to listen to that gossip all night. Maybe I should send out a group text, or email, because it seems like everyone is mad at me these days. I keep fucking up, and I'm at a point in my life where I need to take control back.

My phone beeps, but it's from none of the women I just reached out to.

Dice: You sure know how to make an entrance. Remind me not to invite you to my birthday.

Rhett: Shut up. What happened after I left?

Dice: We all talked shit about you.

Fucker. He sends another text.

Dice: The girls all formed a club. The I Hate Rhett Club. They asked me to join.

Rhett: And did you?

Dice: Yeah, I'm the president.

Rhett: Only president you'll ever be.

Dice: Ouch. Everyone was talking about it all night. You going to bang Natty next and make it three for three?

Why the fuck do I like this guy?

Rhett: Don't think she'd go for it.

Dice: It will blow over. Say sorry. On your knees.

Rhett: Trying.

I thought I'd be on my knees tonight, but for a whole different reason.

Only my mom replies to any of my texts, telling me to come and see her so we can talk about it all. I decide to head back over to the clubhouse to deal with the fallout, and to hopefully clear my name and explain my side of the story. I find Clover in the kitchen, helping tidy up all the beer bottles.

"Where's my goddaughter?" I ask.

She stills at the sound of my voice. "With my parents. Why? You suddenly care about someone other than your own penis?"

I pick up the bottles from the table and start to help her. "Did you get my text?"

"I didn't read it," she replies, lifting her chin up at me. "I'm angry, Rhett. We have a friendship code, and you seem to have forgotten it."

"I didn't know."

She sighs, puts the empty bottles in the recycling bin and turns to me. "You truly didn't know that was Cara's half sister? You had no idea?"

"No."

"Well, you obviously have a type then, don't you?" she replies with a narrowed gaze. "You could have brought any other woman in the world and last night would have gone completely differently. It's not that we don't want you to be happy, and to find someone and fall in love. We just didn't realize it'd be Cara's new sister, who I've been unsure about ever since I met her. And now we find out she's your new woman?"

"That's not fair, Clo. Con is a good person, and she didn't know who I was. It's all a fucked-up coincidence. And you might not trust her, but I do. I vouch for her a hundred percent."

"And how long have you known her exactly to vouch for her?" she asks, raising her brow and looking unamused.

Shit.

"Not that long, but—"

"But you're thinking with your dick, Rhett. If you say you didn't know, I believe you. But do you really think that *she* didn't know?" she asks, studying me.

"She says that she didn't. And yeah, I believe her. From what I saw last night, she really, genuinely cares about Cara. She didn't want anything to do with me after finding out who I was, if that makes you feel any better." Cara must not have mentioned me at all to her.

"Nothing about last night will make me feel better," she grumbles. "I'm sure you can understand it was a shock. It was going to be awkward enough having you and Cara finally in the same room, and then you show up with her sister, who I don't fully trust, if I'm being honest."

"I never knew you were so judgmental, Clo."

"I'm protective."

"You're threatened. I've known you a long time and I am willing to bet you don't trust her because you don't want someone to change what you and Cara have."

I know I struck a nerve when Clover just snorts. "Please. I'm never threatened. Cara is my girl for life."

"But she'll never be your sister. You're being unfair," I say.

"And you obviously haven't known her long, so why are you defending her?" she fires back at me, scowling. "You seem to care more about Con's feelings than Cara's. I might be judgmental and maybe a little threatened, but you are betraying Cara if you keep seeing her sister. Come on, Rhett. If one of my friends dated my brother, Asher, I'd be fucking pissed."

"We. Didn't. Know," I say between clenched teeth.

"Okay, you didn't know. I believe you that this was one big coincidence. But now what? Are you going to keep seeing her?" she asks, pausing and watching me.

I hesitate. "I don't know. She doesn't really want anything to do with me anymore, so probably not."

"Probably not? Wrong answer," she grumbles, shaking her head. "It should be a definite no."

I scrub my hand down my face. "I don't know. Damn it, Clo, I like her. But I don't want to hurt Cara, and I don't want all this drama."

And like I said, Con couldn't get out of my presence any faster if she tried. I'm never bringing a woman to the clubhouse again before doing a full background check and family tree.

Clover sighs and touches my shoulder. "This all needs to die down. You're right, I have had my guard up and I'm being a little more judgmental than usual with Con, because I didn't want her trying to take advantage of Cara. But now that I know she just wants to get to know her sister, I can admit I've been unfair to her."

"She isn't her father," I say gently. "And she really does care about Cara. You should have seen how horrified she was when she found out. She was almost in tears. She said that she didn't want to give you a reason to hate her, and now without even trying she did."

Clover's eyes flash with melancholy. I know she's not a bad person, and she wouldn't want to hurt anyone. She's just extremely loyal to Cara, and if she sees a threat, she will do anything to eliminate it. "I'm sure Cara and Con will sort it out. They are sisters after all."

"I hope so," I reply, opening my arms out to her. "Now, are you going to keep being cold to me? Or are you going to show me just a little bit of the love you show Cara?"

Her lips twitch as she steps into my arms, hugging me tightly. "You know I do love you, Rhett. You've just been making some terrible choices and it's hard to be on your side because of them."

"I know." I sigh, kissing the top of her head. "Trust me, I know. One day I'll tell you everything. But the whole Con thing? That must be my karma because I didn't see it coming. And you know what? I actually *did* like her. She's the first… Never mind."

"First what?" she presses.

"She's the first woman I've slept with sober since Cara. The first one I've actually taken on a date. I like spending time with her, and I like the way I feel when I'm with her," I admit, shrugging.

"Are you sure it wasn't a replacement for Cara? Since they're so similar?"

"I honestly don't think they're similar at all. Sure,

now that I know they're sisters, I can see some resemblance, but Con and I actually have a lot in common."

And a whole different connection. The two can't be compared.

"There are plenty of other women out there. The right one will come along," she says softly.

But what if Con was the right one?

I guess we may never find out.

Chapter Eleven

Con

I leave the hotel and drive home as soon as the sun comes up. When I arrive at my house, I jump straight into bed and just lie there, still processing everything that happened last night.

I sent Cara a text message last night but she didn't reply, so I try to call her but she doesn't pick up. I feel like shit and I need to speak to her so I can make it better. I know she probably needs some time. She and Rhett were obviously once very close, from what I can understand, and their families also all know each other well. I remember her telling me that she had only had one long-term boyfriend before Decker, her childhood love, and now I know that person was Rhett.

Shit.

We might not have grown up together, but apparently we do have the same taste in men.

And ain't that a bitch.

The whole thing is one giant misunderstanding, but it makes me look so bad, and the things that Clover and Natty said to me were so hurtful. Cruel even. I know they were angry and surprised in the moment, but you can't take words back, and I will always think of what they said when I see them.

I'm hurt.

Especially because I'm not that kind of woman. I'd never go against girl code, and I like to think of myself as someone who can be trusted. I've only just gotten Cara into my life and I would never do anything to jeopardize that. I don't think that she knows how truly important she is to me.

I didn't reply to Rhett's text. It wasn't his fault what happened—he didn't know who I was either—but clearly the two of us could have communicated better and if we had, we could have figured this whole thing out before it got to this.

It also means that Cara hasn't really opened up to me much or I'd have known more information about Rhett from her. I guess because I came into her life during her Decker stage, that's all I know and hear about. Rhett was a different chapter for her, and one that I wasn't a part of.

I felt so much happier with Rhett in my life, getting to know him, but now I feel worse than before I met Cara. I'm all the way back at the start, which hurts after making so much progress. Will I lose my job now? Maybe when they hear about what happened, they won't want me there; Cara got me the job after all. I could deal with losing the job, but I couldn't deal with losing her.

All I need is five minutes of her time to explain.

I decide to give her a few days to cool down and then I'll show up at her house and make her listen to me. I don't know how one says sorry for sleeping with an ex, but I'm going to try.

It's all that I can do.

Monday rolls around and I'm looking forward to going to work as a distraction. Rhett doesn't text or call me again, and I think it's because he's realized the same thing I have—we aren't going to work out. It's just not possible, unless Cara is okay with it, and I doubt she's ever going to be.

I do care about him, but Cara comes first. If I had to choose between them, I'd choose my sister every time.

"Good morning," Bronte says to me, smiling as I step into the garage. She acts normal, which makes me think they haven't heard about any of the drama from the weekend. I don't think Cara would ever do that to me, but you never know. I don't know where I stand right now or what she's thinking, and it's making me feel very anxious and on edge. She can take away all that she has given me if she feels like it.

"Good morning." I rest my handbag on my desk and tidy the files there. "Victoria off today?" I ask, referring to the other receptionist that works here.

"Yeah, she's actually got a few days off because she's going away on vacation," Bronte reminds me.

Oh yeah.

I need to focus on work. I'm not someone who is good at pretending that everything is fine when it's not, but I am professional and do my best to act like it's any normal day, and that my heart isn't hurting.

It's hard, but it's called being an adult.

I live my life on autopilot for the next few days. I work as hard as I can, and when I get home I play my guitar, losing myself in music, or I aggressively clean and organize my house. That seems to keep me busy. I wait until Thursday after work when I decide to try to speak to Cara.

I show up at her house with some flowers and a bottle of wine. I realize at the last second that's probably what a cheating man would show up with, but I don't know, I just didn't want to come here empty-handed.

Decker opens the door, eyes widening when he sees me. I stop him before he can say anything. "I know she's mad at me, but I just want to apologize and explain my side of the story to her. So please, let me do that."

He glances into the house and nods. "Okay. She's outside in the garden."

"Thank you," I say, stepping past him and walking through their house and out the back door. I find her sitting on the ground surrounded by seedlings.

"Thirty," I hear her counting, and I realize they must be for school.

"Hey, Cara," I say, making her jump.

She turns around and looks up at me. "Hey, what are you doing here?" She doesn't sound angry, just surprised.

"I was hoping we could talk about what happened. I thought I'd give you a few days to cool down, but it's been hard," I admit, placing the flowers and alcohol down on the grass next to her. "These are for you."

"Con—"

"Just please hear me out, Cara. I didn't know that Rhett was your ex-boyfriend. And he didn't know I was your sister. Half sister, whatever. I'm so sorry, I never would have gone near him if I knew, but I didn't. I've only ever known you as being with Decker. I never saw you with Rhett and I don't think we ever talked about your ex-boyfriend by name. I'm so sorry that I hurt you. I never meant to."

She picks up the sunflowers and stares at them. "I was in shock when I saw the two of you there together, I have to admit. I didn't know what to think, but I did feel betrayed. Rhett is free to move on with his life—I want him to be happy—but never once did I think I'd see him with you."

"I know," I agree, sitting down next to her, legs crossed. "And I never thought I was going to walk into that party and have all of that happen. When I knew he was a biker I should have spoken to you about it; I know you have all those biker ties. But never once did I think..." I trail off and take a deep breath. "I'm sorry. I just want you to know that I would never purposely hurt you. That's not who I am."

"I know," Cara replies, forcing a smile. "And thank you for coming and explaining this to me. To be honest, I'm not angry. I just needed a little time to process it. I know that everyone else is wild about it and expects me to be really hurt, but I think it was more the shock of it all."

"I know it's a little awkward now, but I'm not seeing him anymore. It's all over with. And I'd like it if you could forgive me."

"I forgive you, Con. You didn't even know, so I guess there's nothing to really say sorry for," she says, placing the flowers back down on the grass and studying me. "I'm sorry for what Clover and Natty said to you. I don't know exactly what that was, but Clover did say it wasn't her proudest moment. They shouldn't have spoken to you like that, and I apologize on their behalf."

"They were protecting you," I say, shrugging, but I do appreciate her saying that. Their words did hurt, and I hate that the people who love her see me that way.

I know Rhett wanted to protect her, too. I didn't miss when he let go of me to grab onto Cara. In fact, I keep replaying that part over and over. Will Rhett always love her? I don't know. But the fact that I do resemble Cara a little keeps occupying my mind. Is that why he went for me in the first place? Because I look like Cara? If so, that is really fucked-up, and I can't help but feel used. He never wanted me. He wanted the Wish version of Cara, as Natty put it.

And I guess it's not my problem to concern myself with anymore, because that chapter is now closed.

"I know, but they didn't need to take it that far. We are adults now, and we all need to act like it. And the Rhett and Cara era is over and done with. Rhett is free to make his own choices now. I'm sorry I didn't respond to you earlier, but I am glad you stopped by. Do you want to help me plant a thousand seedlings into pots? They're for a fundraiser at the school."

I exhale in relief and nod. "I'd love to."

I know things won't just go back to the way they were, but at least we have spoken about it, and we can work on our relationship. It's actually weird because Cara seems the least angry about what happened out of everyone. I wish the others around her would follow suit.

And as for Rhett?

I wish I never laid eyes on him.

Chapter Twelve

Rhett

After an hour taking my anger out on the boxing bag, I get dressed to head out with the MC. Arrow has been taking me with him on all of his meetings with other MCs, other chapters of the Wind Dragons and any business associates we have. We discuss business and if there are any problems that are coming up. He only does this quarterly, but it's good for them to see me stepping into his shoes.

Since our chapter of the Wind Dragons has gone straight and does not deal with anything illegal, it's mainly just checking on chapter numbers and if there are any issues that pop up. Soon it will be me interacting with them alone and representing the Wind Dragons, and he wants me to have a good business relationship with everyone involved. It's a lot to take on, but I know this is something that I want to do. I'm proud of my MC, and how it's evolved over the years. And I'm looking forward to where I can take it.

Leah walks out of Dice's room, her long braids dangling down her back. She's dressed in activewear, tight leggings and a crop top, showing off her shapely figure. I try not to look because she's Dice's, but shit, I still have eyeballs.

"What's the update on the drama from the party?" she asks, following me into the kitchen and pulling out a bottle of water.

Leaning against the counter, I cross my arms against my chest. "You coming here to gossip?"

"I'm just asking what everyone wants to," she replies, closing the fridge with her hip and pulling out a chair. "We were all there and saw it play out, so we're all invested."

"There's nothing to report. All the women are pissed at me, as far as I know, and I'm enemy number one," I say, glancing over at her. I need some inside information from the other sex. "You're a woman."

"Very observant."

"What should I do to fix this whole mess?" I ask.

"With Con?" she asks, brows drawing together. "Or with the Natty-Clover-Cara trio?"

"The trio. No, not even the trio, just Cara. She's the one at the center of all of this. And I can't be with Con anyway, so it's probably for the best."

"Why can't you be with her?" Leah asks, taking a sip of water and putting the lid back on the bottle.

"Because it's going to cause more shit, and it will be awkward for Cara."

"So you're more focused on Cara's feelings than Con's?" she asks, nodding to herself. "Interesting."

"What's interesting? It's not that I am more focused on Cara, it's that Con and I aren't seeing each other anymore. And don't use that psychology shit on me."

Leah is a second-year psychology student, and I know she's always analyzing all of us.

She laughs, covering her mouth with her hand. "I'm sorry. I think for Cara you need to seek her out and talk to her in person. You didn't purposely hurt Cara; it's all a big misunderstanding. So clear it up."

I nod. "You're right. I just feel like I keep messing up, it's one thing after another."

"Well, all you can do is learn from it. Can't change what happened now," she replies. "You know, Dice and I work so well because we communicate with each other, and consider each other."

"Yeah, yeah, don't rub your healthy relationship in my face right now," I grumble.

"I'm just saying. You need to work on your communication skills a little. I know you don't want to hear this, but if you spoke to Cara and explained to her how you were feeling, and maybe realized something wasn't working and that's why you stopped coming home to her and treating her how you used to, maybe you could have made that work. Or maybe if you and Con communicated better you could have figured out this connection before you came to the party. You have to open up a little, Rhett. I know you're a man and all, but use your words."

Use my words. Even though Leah doesn't have all the information, she is right. I made all these choices and decisions and never gave Cara an option. And then with Con I didn't want to tell her much about my relationship with Cara, but if I had been honest, maybe she and I could still be together.

"Fuck, you're right. I've kept everything to myself,

and let everyone think shit that didn't even happen, and now I'm the bad guy, all because I couldn't openly communicate how I was feeling," I say.

"What shit didn't even happen?" she asks, brows furrowing.

I study her for a few seconds, realizing my misstep. But if I'm going to follow Leah's advice, then I need to start being honest. "You know how Cara thinks I cheated on her? I didn't. I'd never cheat on her. But I also knew that we weren't going to work, and that the life of an old lady wasn't for her, so I just let her believe…"

"You took the easy way out and let her think you cheated so she'd dump you and you wouldn't have to be honest with her?" she asks, and I can hear the judgment in her tone, and see it in her expression.

"Yes, I mean, I did kiss the girl when I knew she was looking," I admit, cringing. "So I guess that would count as cheating, technically, but that's all that happened. And I did it on purpose. And you're the only one who knows the truth. I didn't tell a single soul. Wow, you really are going to make a great shrink." I just opened up to her. What a fucking miracle worker she is.

Her jaw drops open as she processes the information I just dumped on her. "I can't believe you'd hurt her like that and let her think that you cheated on her. Are you going to tell her the truth or continue to be a coward?"

Ouch. "What's the point? It's old news now. She has moved on and I don't think we need to revisit the past."

"What about your reputation? Do you know how much it hurts being cheated on? She didn't deserve that, Rhett. I think you should tell her the truth."

I knew she was going to say that. Hell, even I know it's the right thing to do. "I don't care about my reputation, Leah. I'm a biker, and I'm about to become president."

"Yeah, okay, I get that," she replies, frowning. "But you have to care what the people who love you think about you."

Of course I fucking do. But like I said, it's in the past now, and it won't change anything.

Dice steps into the room, saving me from replying. "There you are."

"She's giving me a free therapy session."

Dice grins, walks over to Leah and kisses her on top of her head. "She's good at that. I'm heading out with the MC—you going to stay here or you heading home?"

"I'm going for a run, then I'll go home," she says. The two of them then start whispering to each other, and kissing, so I quietly leave the room, thinking about what she just said.

Communication.

Honesty.

Things I clearly need to work on.

"When are we heading off?" I ask Arrow when I find him outside, standing next to his motorcycle.

"An hour or two. Why?"

"Do you need me? I want to drop by Cara's house."

"All right," he replies, tone unimpressed. "We will leave without you. But don't make this a habit."

"I won't."

I decide it is time to have the conversation with Cara that I have been avoiding for so long. If I want to move forward and actually have a friendship with her and

Clover, I need to lay it all out on the table. She deserves that much, and I know this; I've just been blocking it all out instead of dealing with it, which wasn't the right way to handle it. I can imagine how hurt, confused and angry she's going to be. But it's better that she knows.

As I ride over to her home, I can't believe this is where I am—driving over to Cara's house where she lives with another man. I never in a million years would've expected this is how things would play out with us. It just proves that I do need to have this conversation and I really have to let go of the past.

"Hey," I say as she opens the door dressed in her robe. Her hair is in two long braids, and she is fresh-faced like she's just out of the shower.

"Rhett? Is everything okay?" she asks, brow furrowed in concern.

"Yeah, I'm sorry for just dropping by, but I wanted to talk to you if you have a few minutes."

"Of course," she says instantly, opening the door wider to welcome me inside.

And here is the woman who is one of my best friends. She's always been there when I need her, and even now when we aren't on good terms, she is still here for me.

I follow her inside and we both sit down in her living room. "Can I get you something to drink?"

I shake my head. I need to get this all out before it eats at me from the inside out. "No thank you. I just need to be honest with you about everything, and I know you're going to be fucking angry…"

She gives me one of her *Seriously, Rhett?* faces. It's a mixture between a smirk and a frown. "What else could there be? If I'm still talking to you after you cheated on me and then slept with my sister, I don't think there is much more for me to get angry at."

I shift on her leather couch. "I first want to say that I never knew Con was your sister. I'd never purposely hurt you, Cara, or do something so low."

She stays silent, and I know that she must be thinking about me cheating on her, and how much that hurt.

"I also need to admit something else about our breakup…"

She stays silent which is probably worse because that just means I have to keep talking.

"I never cheated on you."

Her eyes widen, confusion filling her brown eyes. I know she's thinking about the kiss she saw. And now that I look at her, I realize she and Con do have the same eyes. I honestly didn't even remember what Cara's eyes looked like until now, probably because I was avoiding looking at her in the eye for months as I let my ruse play out.

She opens her mouth, but I continue before she does. "I mean, I did kiss Trisha, but only because I knew you were there. I know that it doesn't make it any better, but that was the one and only kiss we ever shared, and the only time I've ever done something like that. I was dealing with some things, which caused me to be out more. You've accused me of cheating in the past and I decided to use that to push you away instead of telling you how I really felt."

I can tell she's processing everything I'm saying, so I keep going. "When they told me they wanted me to be president of the MC, I was happy, but I also knew you did not want to be stuck in the same clubhouse for the rest of your life. I knew you were made for a different life. And you deserved that."

She wraps her arms around herself in a protective position, making me feel like even more shit. "You have got to be shitting me. This is too much to process."

"Take your time."

"Don't you dare tell me what to do." Her words are like a whip, slashing at my skin. I feel the sting. "Let's take this one thing at a time. So you decided, on your own, that because you didn't think I wanted to be the president's old lady, you'd sabotage our relationship?"

Shit, that does sound bad when she phrases it like that. I just nod.

"I think that was my decision to make, Rhett. Not yours."

"I—" I try to respond, but she just holds up her hand so I don't say another word.

"And then, instead of having the balls to just break up with me, you let me believe you were cheating on me so I'd break up with you?"

Fuck. This is not going the way I planned. I nod again, staying quiet this time.

"What the fuck is wrong with you?"

I don't know whether I should start talking yet, so I just look at her.

"You can talk now!" she says, obviously exasperated with me.

"I don't know what I was thinking. I just remember back to that time we were hiding out together when all that shit went down, and you said you didn't want this biker life and you didn't want our future children to have to do this either. I thought I was doing the right thing."

"The right thing? First of all, you didn't even give me a choice. There was no conversation, no asking my opinion. You made a decision for me." She holds up a second finger, which means I'm in for a list of things. "Second, and I think this is more telling than anything, *you chose the MC over me!*"

At her scream, Decker, who I forgot lives here, comes into the living room looking between the two of us. He must have just come out of the shower at that moment, because he's butt fucking naked. "What the hell is going on?"

"I'm sorry. I didn't mean to show up at your house, but I needed to talk to Cara…" I avert my eyes to the ceiling.

Well, we now know what Cara sees in him.

"I'm not embarrassed, but I'll put on clothes so you don't get a crick in your neck." I hear him leave and then he comes back shortly with sweats on.

"Go ahead, tell him. Tell him what you just told me." Cara swings her arm from me to him.

"Please tell me you did not sleep with Natty," he says, a look of horror on his face. But in that moment, both Cara and I crack up laughing.

I shake my head. "No, never."

Cara tries to control herself. "No, babe, basically he just told me that he never cheated on me and wanted me to break up with him so he didn't have to break up with me, all because he wanted to be president of the Wind Dragons and knew I wouldn't be happy as an old lady."

Decker gives me a *what the fuck* look, and honestly,

I'm right there with him. "Okay, don't hate me here, but isn't that true, Cara? You never wanted to really be ingrained in the MC. You told me that very early in our relationship," he says. I give him a mental fist bump.

"That's not the point! He didn't talk to me about it and he didn't let me make a decision. And he was a coward and made me break up with him."

"Okay, okay." Decker holds his hands up in surrender. "While that was not a great move, Cara, didn't it work out the way it was supposed to? You and me would have never gotten together if he didn't make that decision." Okay, maybe he isn't that bad.

She takes a deep breath. "Look, I get what you're saying. Rhett and I were drifting apart, hanging on to what was and our history. He was too busy with the club and not coming home, and I was just alone most of the time. But I wish we'd had this conversation instead of him letting me think that he cheated on me. That really hurt me."

Am I even part of this conversation anymore?

"Can I say something?" I raise my hand, feeling like I'm interrupting my mom and dad. "I know the way things happened was not the best way to handle this. If I could go back in time, I would've been way more up front. Cara…" I turn to look at her directly. "You are right—I wanted president more. It hurts me to admit that to you, but I never even fathomed giving up the opportunity to become president of the MC. So yes, Decker," I turn to him now. "You're also right. I do think it worked out the way it was supposed to because Cara should always be number one with any man she is with. She and I will always be our first loves, but we are not meant to be together."

I look back at Cara and give her a hopeful smile. "You're my best friend and I see how happy you are with this guy." I point my thumb over at Decker. "I may have been butthurt about it, but now that you know the truth, I really would like to move forward and go back to being best friends."

Cara gives a small shake of her head and her *Seriously, Rhett?* face. "You're still one of my closest friends and always will be. But you hurt me by letting me think you would cheat on me. You let everyone think you were this horrible person. Was it really worth it?"

I scratch the back of my head not knowing how to answer. I shrug. "I made my bed, now I have to lie in it. I am sorry," I say. "There's no excuse. I was an idiot and just not thinking right. I'm sorry I hurt you, Cara."

"Thank you for coming and telling me the truth," she says, nodding. "It was hard, but I needed to hear this. I wish we had this conversation earlier, but better late than never. But before we make up and sing 'Kumbaya,' can I ask a question? What about Con?"

The sound of her name is like a bucket of ice flowing over me. "What about her? We're not seeing each other anymore."

Cara stares at me. "Is she just a hookup? Or do you really like her?"

"Way to put me on the spot…" I debate how honest I want to be, but if I learned anything from this whole thing, it's that I probably should just be honest. "She wasn't just a hookup. I like her. We have a lot in common."

"If she wasn't my sister, would you want to date her? Be in a relationship with her?"

"Shit, I don't know, Cara. Why does it matter? We aren't going to see each other anymore."

"Just answer the question, Rhett. You owe me that much." I wonder how long she'll use what I did as guilt. Probably the rest of my life.

"Yeah, we were spending a lot of time together. I mean, it was casual, but I could see myself dating her."

Cara is quiet for a long time and then looks at Decker. They do this weird thing where they just stare at each other for what seems like forever, but really must be ten seconds. It's like they are having a conversation with one another silently.

"If you like her and she is not just a hookup, then I think you should date her."

"I'm sorry, what?" I must not have heard her right.

"You have my blessing to date her."

"But she's your sister!" I feel like I walked into another dimension here. Between me starting to like Decker and now Cara telling me to date Con, I don't know what is going on.

"So what? Yeah, it was awkward at first, but you and I are friends. Best friends. And I've moved on and am with Decker. Why shouldn't you and Con have what he and I have? I'm not going to stand in the way of love just because it's awkward."

"I'm sure Clover will have something to say about it."

"Let me handle Clover. You and Con both deserve happiness, and if it's together, even better."

"You're fucking weird, you know that?" I say.

Cara laughs and walks me to the door. Before I leave,

she gives me a big hug. "I want what's best for you, Rhett. Always."

Fuck.

I walk away feeling emotional, confused…

And fucking happy.

It's been a while since I've spent some time with my goddaughter, and Clover said I'm welcome to drop in whenever I like. On the way to their house I stop and pick up some age-appropriate toys and pink roses for Sapphire. Never too young to set the standard.

Clover is standing out the front of her house when I pull up on the bike, her phone in her hand. "What are you doing?" I ask when I remove my helmet and turn the engine off.

"Taking a video."

"Of me?" I ask, confused.

"No, of me." She rolls her eyes and comes over. Of course it was of her. "I made some lunch, so I hope you are hungry."

"Where's Fire?"

She turns and points to a corner of the garden where Fire is sitting playing with some toys. I reach into my satchel and pull out everything I got for her, even though the flowers are slightly crushed from being in my bag.

Clover gasps. "Awww. That's pretty cute, Rhett. You trying to get some brownie points?"

"Hey, you all might hate me, but Fire never will," I reply with a grin, walking over to her and sitting next to her. "Hello, beautiful, look what Uncle Rhett got you," I say to her.

She looks up at me and smiles widely. I hand her

the flowers, and she takes them, the bouquet almost covering her whole face. She then laughs and throws them on the ground, and comes over to me and gives me a big hug.

I melt. "You are so cute, you know that? I brought you some toys."

"Toys?"

I nod, and lay down the doll, soft toy and bubbles on the grass. "What do you think?"

"Bubbles!"

Clover comes and sits next to us. "You brought her flowers. She's not even two yet. I don't know why I find that so adorable, but I do."

"I should have brought you some, too."

"You should have," she replies in a dry tone. "What's been happening with you? I heard you are overseeing Toxic." Toxic is part of a chain of strip clubs the MC owns.

"Yeah, I was there last night. It's doing pretty well."

Clover nods. "People like boobs and ass."

I laugh. "They do."

"I went and saw Con at work the other day," she says, surprising me. "I apologized for what happened at the clubhouse and gave her some doughnuts. I figured that everyone likes doughnuts."

"Clover Black apologized out of her own free will? Holy fuck, I bet it rains today."

"It's Clover Banks," she reminds me, like I could forget. "And I'm older now, more mature and less stub-born."

I arch my brow at her, and she ducks her head sheepishly. "Unless you come for my friends or family. But I was wrong, and I said sorry."

"That was nice of you," I say, feeling proud. "You know she's not the bad guy you have painted her out to be."

"I'm slowly seeing that," she agrees, kissing Sapphire's head when she comes within reach. "Do you guys still talk?"

"Sometimes."

She studies me for a long second. "Do you think that's a good idea?"

No, probably not. "Yeah, why not? I'm friends with lots of women."

"Who you've slept with?" she asks, sounding skeptical.

"Yes. Cara, for one," I point out. "Actually, come to think of it, I think you're my only female friend I *haven't* slept with."

She scrunches her nose. "Well, at least I have some taste."

"You keep me humble, Clo."

She laughs. "Someone has to. Can't have you walking about thinking you are the shit. Especially as future MC president. You're going to have women throwing themselves at you without you even having to try."

"I already don't have to try—"

"Shut up."

Fire decides to copy her mom. "Shut up, shut up!"

I shake my head at Clover. "Now look what you have done. Don't listen to your mom, Fire, she's a bad influence."

Clover laughs. "I'm raising a little version of me. Do you know how scary that is?"

"I'm sure your mom felt the same way," I reply with a smirk. "There's actually something I wanted to talk to you about."

"What is it?" she asks, stilling. "What else did you do?"

"This time it's not what I did, it's more what I didn't do," I say, taking a deep breath before continuing. "I never cheated on Cara. I mean, I kissed Trisha, only because I knew Cara would see and end it with me. She assumed I was sleeping with her, and I let her think that."

Her eyes widen. "What? Rhett, why would you do that?"

"Well—"

She cuts me off before I can begin to explain. "You're telling me that you're not with Cara right now by choice? You didn't want to be with her?"

"Clover—"

"This is somehow even worse than the cheating!"

I can't win.

"Let me explain," I demand. I tell her everything I told Cara, actually surprised Cara hasn't told her herself.

When I finish, Clover looks exhausted. Imagine how I feel. "Rhett, that was…"

"Heroic? Admirable?" I say jokingly.

"So freaking stupid."

"I know, I know. But it is what happened and no use trying to change it. It is what it is." I look at Fire, who has been sitting quietly playing. "Fire, do you want to come with me to put these flowers in some water?"

Fire nods and takes my hand, the two of us heading inside. Clover follows behind us. I find a vase in the kitchen and fill it with water while Fire watches me. "Okay, you hold the flowers and hand me one at a time, okay?"

We eventually get them all in there, and I place it on the table. "There, beautiful."

"Rhett—"

"I know how much of a mess this is, Clo, trust me. I'm a shit person for doing it, but I'm trying to change."

Clover goes quiet.

"Shit," Fire decides to say, copying me.

I wince. "I said sit, not shit."

"Shit," she repeats with a grin. Yeah, this kid is trouble. But I wouldn't expect anything else from a spawn of Clover.

"And how does Con fit into all of this?" Clover asks, studying me.

"I like Con. I don't know, we just connected. We have a lot in common. She's strong—"

"Cara is strong," she defends.

I drop my head. "Clo, you have to stop this. How are me and Cara going to move on if you keep doing this? You have to stop meddling. You have to stop letting your opinions on what our lives should be come out."

Clover looks like I've slapped her.

"I'm sorry. I didn't mean that to come out so harsh, Clo. But why are you trying to push Cara on me? She's with Decker."

Clover sighs. "You're right. I'm not trying to do that. It's instinct, I think?"

"Do you talk about how wonderful I am to Cara? That maybe she should leave Decker for me?"

Clover snorts. "No way. Cara is the happiest she's ever been." There was a time that statement would've hurt, but now I just agree with her. Is this called being an adult?

"So why can't you let me find that?" I ask without looking at her.

Clover doesn't say anything for a long time. The only sound is Fire kicking her feet and humming. "I... You... There is no excuse. I am sorry, Rhett. You're one hundred percent right."

I turn and give her a hug. "I know what I did was wrong. I know I didn't make the right choices. But it is what happened and beating me up for it is not helping. I beat myself up over it. But you know, I've come to realize that everything happened the way it was supposed to."

"And Con?"

I give a long sigh. "I haven't figured that out yet. She really made it a point to say she would not date me even if Cara was fine with it, which she is, by the way. She told me that when I told her the truth."

"I guess I really don't give Con credit, do I?"

"You never do," I say with a laugh.

"And you think Con could be an old lady to a president of a motorcycle club? You think she could lead? Be trusted? Be the heart of the Wind Dragons?" she asks, and for once I don't hear sarcasm in her voice. She's genuinely asking me this.

"I don't know, okay? But my gut tells me yes. She

cares about people. She doesn't judge anyone. And the MC is a family. That's all she's ever wanted."

She stares into my eyes quietly for a few moments, reading me. She's always been able to read me.

"Thank you for being honest with me," she finally says, and then thankfully changes the subject. "Now, are you hungry? We should eat. Food fixes everything."

Chapter Thirteen

Con

When Jamie tells me she got engaged to a man she only just met a few weeks ago, I don't think it's the best of ideas, but who am I to judge her? I'm the girl who slept with her sister's ex. So I smile, congratulate her and agree to attend her last-minute bachelorette party the following weekend.

I wear a little black dress, as requested by the bride-to-be, and meet her at my old job where we have dinner and a few drinks before heading next door to Toxic, the strip club, even though I don't love coming here. It's weird knowing that once upon a time my mom worked here, and it's not a place I enjoy being at, but I try to have a good time for Jamie. Tonight is about her, not me.

"Are there any male strippers here?" Jamie's sister, Kylie, asks me.

"I don't think so. Unless the place has changed."

"Jason didn't want her having any male strippers, but he said females were okay, so here we are," Clarissa, Jamie's cousin, comments.

I think that's a red flag, but okay. Again, I miss many

red flags myself when they are waving right in my face, so I can't really talk.

We all sit down at a booth right in front of the stage and watch as the women come out and dance. Trays of alcohol are put in front of us on the table, and I think okay, why not? I deserve to have a good night.

"To the bride-to-be!" I say, tequila shot lifted in the air.

The alcohol keeps flowing, and as my head gets blurrier, I feel free. Happy. Even if it's only temporary. We all make sure to tip the strippers well. A beautiful blonde leans down and tells us how much fun she's having dancing for us, which makes us all cheer loudly. I get up from the booth, the alcohol hitting me harder than I realized, and make my way to the bathroom. I'm halfway there when someone grabs my arm, stopping me from moving.

"Hey, what are you doing here?"

I turn and stare into Rhett's beautiful blue eyes, and then lower my gaze onto his lips. They are good lips. His cheeks are covered in stubble, and his long hair is down and around his face. "You are a good-looking man, you know that?"

"How much have you had to drink?" he asks, brow furrowing.

"A lot. And I'm here having a good time. What are *you* doing here?" I ask, poking him in his hard chest. It suddenly hits me that he's at a strip club, staring at sexy women dancing, and I can't help but feel annoyed. "Picking up your latest fling for the night? Just a heads-up, maybe warn her before you bring her to meet your ex-girlfriend this time."

He winces, but sighs and lets go of my arm. I miss his touch instantly. "I'm sorry, I should have told you. Come on, let me get you some water."

I roll my eyes. "I don't want any water. Please, go and enjoy your night. Pretend I don't exist. You're good at it."

I step into the ladies' bathroom and slam the door behind me. I step in front of the mirror and stare at my reflection for a moment. "Don't let him ruin your night."

Why is my heart racing at the mere sight of him?

I hate that I feel like this, that Rhett has this control over me.

I hate that I want him even though I have to stay away.

By the time I come out, Rhett is sitting at the bar, and I avoid looking in his direction and head back to our booth, where Jamie is now getting a lap dance. I sit down and pick up another shot. Yeah, not the best idea, but I need one.

Fuck it.

It doesn't take long before he comes over, and all the women cheer like he's the male stripper we've all been waiting for.

"I'll take a lap dance from him," Kylie comments, and I turn to her with a narrowed gaze.

Rhett sits down next to me and hands me a bottle of water. "Drink some water, please."

"I'm fine," I tell him. "I can handle my alcohol. And I'm also not your problem. So please let me enjoy my night with my friends."

I can feel his eyes on me. "You look good."

My head snaps to him, and I can see and feel the heat

in his eyes. "Don't you even start that shit. And don't look at me like that."

"Like what?"

"Like you want me," I say as I clench my teeth.

"Wanting you isn't the problem here, trust me," he says, moving closer so our legs are touching. "You know what the problem is."

"Don't refer to my sister as a problem," I snap.

He scrubs his hand down my face. "That's not what I meant."

"Oh, that's right, the problem is you actually want Cara but can't have her so you decided to have me instead."

His jaw drops. "That's not what happened, and you know it."

"I look similar to her, Rhett. What else do you think drew you to me? And don't even think about lying to me right now—"

"Okay, yeah, you both have brown hair and eyes. So what? I obviously have a type. But you are nothing like Cara. The reasons why I like you have nothing to do with that," he replies, cupping my cheek with his palm. "*You* are beautiful, *you* are funny. You are stubborn, and real, and have a dry sense of humor that I fucking love. You are a fighter. You are strong. You are sexy as fuck and the two of us have so much chemistry that I literally get hard at the thought of you."

The music goes silent for a second while they change songs, so what he says next can be heard by everyone around us.

"None of that has anything to do with Cara!"

I can feel all eyes on us.

A man walks over and speaks to Rhett. "Sir, we are having an issue outside that needs your attention."

"I'll be there in a second," Rhett tells the man.

"Why is he coming to you?" I ask him quietly. "Do you work here?"

"The MC owns Toxic. We always have," he explains, standing up. He looks me in the eye and demands, "Don't go anywhere, you hear me?"

Great, so the MC used to be my mom's boss.

Just when I think this situation can't get any worse.

He saunters off and of course I'm not going to listen to him. So I get up and am about to walk out when I realize that I'm not ready to go home yet and I shouldn't just leave just because he told me not to. I'm going to stay until the party is over. I just relocate to the bar because I'm petty and moving a few steps is still moving. I'm not listening to anything Rhett has to say. He's not my man, and I'm not his woman.

"Can I buy you a drink?" a man next to me at the bar asks.

I turn to look at him. He's about my age and decent looking, but I still decline. I'm not in the position to be accepting drinks from strangers. "No thank you, I'm okay."

"What's your name?" he asks, facing me with his elbow resting on the bar.

I'm still thinking about Rhett and don't really want to have small talk with this stranger, and I'm about to rejoin the girls at our table when Rhett comes back in and scowls when he spots me. He storms over and stands behind me, staring the man down.

"Get the fuck away from her if you want to live," he says through clenched teeth.

The man backs away with his hands up in front of him, showing his submission. Rhett stares him down until he eventually walks out of Toxic, deciding to go somewhere safer.

I turn around and ask him in a dry tone, "Was that really necessary?" I stare up into his eyes, challenging him. I even go up on my toes to make myself look a little taller. "What if I wanted to talk to him?"

His jaw is tighter than I've ever personally seen it, and his blue eyes flash with anger and…regret? "Don't make this harder than it needs to be."

I can't help it, I glance down at his crotch at the word *hard*, but then quickly look away when I realize what I'm doing.

"Con—" he warns.

He reaches out and tries to touch me, but I back away.

"I can't," I say, and return to the booth. I'm not going to do this.

Even drunk, I'm not going to cross that line with him.

The first time I didn't know, but now I do, and if I do this I'm making a choice to betray Cara.

And I can't do that.

Chapter Fourteen

Rhett

Sitting at the bar, I close my eyes and take a deep breath, silently praying for a break. What are the chances that Con would come to Toxic on the same night as me? The world is playing with me, and someone is having a big fucking laugh right now at my expense. There was the emotional conversation I had with Cara yesterday, and tonight I run into Con.

She's the biggest temptation, in her little black dress and the red lipstick that drives me insane. Why can't I be with her again? Cara did give me her approval, but it still feels…wrong. But when I saw her talking to another man, I felt my blood boil, and I had to stop myself from making an even bigger scene. Which isn't fair to her, I know, but I can't help how I feel.

It's all messed up, and I don't know how to handle this situation. Con obviously knows where she stands; she won't even let me touch her tonight. She is choosing Cara, which is ironic because I couldn't. I chose the club.

Now she's back at her table, laughing and drinking with her friends while I'm sitting at the bar, scowling and watching her every move, wondering how the hell I'm supposed to just walk away from her tonight. I watch as one of the strippers, Cherry, pulls Con onstage and starts to dance with her. I glance around and look out as the other men watch Con dancing to "Pony" by Ginuwine, and grit my teeth, jealous that others are getting to see her this way. This should have been a private show for me and me only, yet all the men here are going to go home and jack off to Con.

Nope.

When she lifts herself up on the pole and starts to spin around, her dress riding up and showing off the edge of her panties, I've had enough. I walk over, trying to contain my anger, and simply carry her off the stage and into one of the empty private rooms.

"What the hell do you think you're doing?" I ask, placing her down on the seat and watching as she scrambles to cover her ass with the material of her dress.

"What am I doing? What do you think *you're* doing?" she replies, standing up and pushing against my chest. I don't move. Which makes her angrier. "I can do whatever I want, Rhett. Don't try to control me."

"You don't care if your dress was riding up to your neck and all the pervy men in the club can see that?" I probe, shaking my head. "You've had too much to drink, Con. You should just go home. Come on, I'll take you there now."

"I'll go home when I'm ready to go home," she declares, lifting her chin. "And I'll get right back on that stage and continue to have a fun night. You should go and do the same."

"Yeah, fine. Go back up there. Like mother like daughter, right?"

She stills, gasps and then slaps me across the face before walking out.

I touch my cheek, gritting my teeth.

Yeah, I deserved that one. I shouldn't have said that, it wasn't fair.

I wait a few seconds and then go after her. I'm playing with fire right now, but I at least want to make sure that she gets home safe. If I dropped her home I would simply get her tucked safely in bed with some water and painkillers and leave.

When I go and look for her, she's not back at the booth, though, or at the bar.

"She left," Jamie says, narrowing her eyes at me. "Don't you hurt her any more than you already have."

"I'm trying," I mutter under my breath as I walk outside, looking around until I spot her across the road, on her phone, probably trying to call a car. She's taken her shoes off and is holding them in her arms. I think that's the universal sign for when a woman is good and ready to go home.

I quickly cross and almost laugh at her expression when she sees me. Yeah, she's pissed.

In more ways than one.

"Come on, I'm taking you home," I say, pointing to my car. Luckily I didn't bring the bike tonight because I had to bring in some alcohol for the bar. I step closer to her. "And I'm sorry for what I said back there. I didn't mean it. I'm an asshole and seeing another guy with you made me mad. But let me at least get you home safely, all right?"

She sighs. "Fine."

Relief fills me, and we both walk to my car side by side, her shoes dangling from her fingers. I open the passenger door for her and she slides in, sitting there with her arms crossed, so I lean over and put her seat belt on for her too, noticing her sweet smell despite all the alcohol she's had. No one can say that I'm not a gentleman.

I hop in and then make my way to her house, the silence between us deafening. The thick air speaks for itself—she's angry and hurt and I'm confused, and the last thing I want to do is hurt her any more than I have.

But I also want her.

And despite Cara giving me her blessing, I don't think Con will give me a chance and it's made me want her even more.

"Do you want me to stop and get you something to eat?" I ask.

She hesitates, but then replies, "No thank you."

"Are you just saying that because you're stubborn but don't want to admit that you want food?" I ask, amused.

Her stomach grumbles, giving me the answer.

I laugh and make a turn to the nearest drive-through window. "What would you like?"

"Cheeseburger and fries would be a treat right now," she says, pulling out money from her wallet.

I ignore her attempts to pay and order what she requested, plus a soda and extra food for me, and then head back to her house. She unlocks the door and we both go inside. She turns the lights on and I set up the food on the table.

"Why did I do shots tonight? That was a terrible

idea," she grumbles, taking a sip of her soda and sitting down at the table. "And why did you have to be there tonight?"

I asked myself the same question. "Maybe fate has other ideas for us."

She lifts those brown eyes up to me and takes a bite of her burger. "Fate is a bitch."

My lip twitches. She's not wrong.

"I like you, Con—"

"I think we should just be friends," she blurts out.

"Friends?" I reply, not liking the way the word tastes on my tongue. But that's how I painted this to Clo, so I guess I was kind of thinking the same way. But to hear her actually say it, yeah, it fucking sucks.

"Yes, friends. It's clear this isn't going to work out, but we keep running into each other. So I feel like it's the best option."

Friends is the last thing I want to be with her, but I can't ask her to put me before Cara. Cara may have given me her blessing, but that is between sisters. And I only want Con to be with me if she wants to be with me, not because of Cara.

"Do you think we could be friends?" I ask.

"Yes, I do," she replies, nodding.

"Okay, friends it is then."

Is it what I want?

No.

But I'll take what I can get…for now.

We eat, and then Con has a shower while I clean up the mess and get her some painkillers and water, and then I tuck her in. She puts on a full tracksuit, and I take the hint. She means it—she wants to be friends, and friends only.

She smiles at me and says good-night.

Fuck.

She's beautiful.

I don't know what it is about her, but there's just something magnetic.

She's a handful, but I like that. I don't care how much attitude she gives me, I find it amusing, and it keeps things interesting and never boring.

"Good night," I say to her as I leave.

"Thank you for getting me home."

I lock the front door and lean back on it, looking out at my car.

There's nothing I want more right now than to climb into that bed and hold her in my arms all night, but instead I get into my car and drive back to the clubhouse.

I'd like to commend myself on my willpower, but the truth is if she gave me the word I'd be in there with her.

But her loyalty to Cara has won out, and I have to respect that.

But if it was up to me, I know where I'd be.

Chapter Fifteen

Con

If I ever had any proof to show that I love Cara, last night would be it. I wanted to ask Rhett to stay so badly, but I couldn't do that.

It doesn't matter what I want, I just need to do the right thing. I'm glad he accepted my offer to be just friends. I mean, it sucks, but that's life.

As I lie in bed nursing a headache and regretting the tequila last night, a knock at the door gets me out of bed. When I find a deliveryman standing there with a bag of food, I'm confused.

"Oh, I didn't order anything," I tell him, brow furrowing.

He glances at the receipt. "Are you Constance Wilder?"

I nod. He passes me the bag and a coffee. "Then this is for you."

He walks away, and I head back inside with a bag of delicious-smelling greasy food. My phone beeps with a text message.

Rhett: Hope the food helps with your hangover.

Con: You didn't have to do that, but thank you.

Why does he have to be so sweet? It's really not helping the situation. He should just be a jerk and make it
easier for me.

I get back into bed and eat the hash browns and ba-
con-and-egg sandwich he sent me. My phone beeps
again, but instead of a text from Rhett, it's from Cara.

Cara: What are you doing today? Want to grab some
lunch and hang out?

I put my phone down, roll over and sigh. I do want to
see her, but at the same time I don't. I just want to chill
in bed and feel sorry for myself, not see my sister and
make it more awkward when I tell her that I saw Rhett
again last night and that he brought me home.

Con: I'm hungover and dying. Rain check?

Cara: No problem! Let me know if you need anything.

Great, now she's been sweet too, which makes me
feel extra guilty. I decide I need a distraction from
Rhett, from the whole situation, and maybe even a break
from my phone.

I don't know…something just has to change.

Two weeks pass, and Rhett and I stick to my whole idea
of just being friends. I'm not going to lie, it's hard for
many reasons. We have the chemistry and the physi-
cal and emotional connection right there, so being only

friends means ignoring that and just living in denial. He hasn't exactly made it easy either. He has kept on asking me out to lunch and dinners as friends, which I agree to, but then his blue eyes contradict everything. He looks at me like he wants me.

I hope I'm not as transparent.

Who am I kidding? I totally am. Our texts get a little bit too flirty for friends, and he mentions needing a cold shower. I turn my head as I see some car lights in my driveway. Frowning, I open the window and see a taxi pull up. Rhett gets out of the passenger side.

What the hell?

I open the door as he staggers up my driveway. "What are you doing here?"

He looks confused for a second, blue eyes narrowed. "I don't know. The driver asked me where my home was."

My brow furrows. "And you decided that was here?"

He nods and grins. "Yes, wherever you are."

Oh. Fuck.

I let him in and he barely makes it to the couch before he falls onto it. I get him some water and make him swallow it down. "Why are you so drunk?"

He sighs. "Probably because I haven't had a drink in so long, and then all the girls at Toxic made me do shots with them and got me fucked-up."

I purse my lips, the euphoria from his previously sweet comments diminished. "You got drunk with some other women and then decided to drop into my house unannounced?"

Because home is wherever I am, apparently.

"Yeah, friends do that," he rationalizes, adjusting

a pillow underneath his neck. "Can I stay here? Or do you want me to leave?"

"You can stay here," I say. I mean, how can I tell him to get out? "Do you want to sleep in the guest room?"

"I'm okay here," he replies, closing his eyes. I get a blanket and cover him up with it, and leave a bottle of water with some Tylenol next to it.

He's going to need that.

Rhett showing up here unexpectedly is like a sign that maybe I should just allow myself to be with him. It's just going to be really hard to get the words out without feeling like I'm doing something wrong.

I guess it's a problem for tomorrow, though, when he is sober.

I save half my dinner for Rhett in case he gets hungry, and then jump into the shower, wondering how the hell I keep getting into these situations. I understand he had a little much to drink, but why would he come here now? When my body is craving his.

We're playing a real dangerous game because we obviously can't stay away from each other.

He came here, he shouldn't have.

I let him stay, I shouldn't have.

He said I was home.

Me, a person, not a place. Me.

How could I not melt at that?

I turn the water off and grab my fluffy white towel, wrapping it around me and looking in the mirror.

Who am I?

Brown hair, guilty brown eyes, and a heart that wants someone it shouldn't.

When I open the bathroom door with the towel

wrapped around me, Rhett's standing there looking a lot more sober than he was a few minutes ago.

"Everything okay?" I ask.

"Con, you don't know what you do to me..." He starts inching closer, and before I know what I'm doing I find myself moving toward him. Like we're two magnets being drawn together.

"Friends can touch, right?" His finger traces the top of my towel; his touch pebbles my skin.

I nod, unable to speak.

He leans down and kisses the inside of my neck. "And friends can give little kisses?"

I can feel him pause, waiting for my permission, which I give him. I can feel my legs shake.

His finger flicks at my towel and it falls to the floor. "Oops."

He bends to pick it up, but instead of standing back up he just looks at me from his knees, his head level with my navel. I instinctively move closer to him.

His hand moves up my thigh and finds the spot between my legs that has been throbbing for him. "Con... tell me you want me the way I want you."

I can barely breathe, let alone speak, so I do what I can. I put my hand over his and start to move it. I tried hard to be a good sister. But the need for Rhett is too powerful.

I come while staring into his eyes. Before I can fall to the floor in bliss, he picks me up and takes me to the bedroom, where he proceeds to show me every way he does not want to be my friend anymore.

I remember going to sleep completely satiated but worried about what this means.

And in the morning he must be thinking the same thing, because he's gone.

I get up for work and show up in my favorite pair of black slacks with a white blouse. I didn't really own any appropriate clothes for this job, so I bought some professional outfits and I've grown to love them. Paired with some block heels and nude lipstick, I kind of look like I have my life together.

We all know how looks can be deceiving.

"You look nice today," Atlas comments when I step into the garage, coffee in hand.

I pause and study him. "Okay, what do you want?"

"Nothing." He smirks, blue eyes amused. "How are you?"

It takes me a moment, but then I realize what this is all about. "You heard about all the drama, didn't you?"

"I hear a lot of things." He nods. "But yes, I did hear about you and Rhett. Don't you think it's ironic? The Forgotten Children drove you off the road because they thought you were Cara, and they were trying to get her to hurt Rhett. And now you and Rhett are having a thing—"

I groan. I forgot about the Forgotten Children, no pun intended. A while back Cara was being threatened by a local gang because of her relationship with Rhett, I guess, and they thought I was her, so they followed me. Cara and I had just entered each other's lives and I didn't really know much; Cara wanted to keep me safe and I never asked any details. But the irony is real.

"We aren't having a thing. We were, and now it's all over," I say, sitting down at my desk, thoughts of last night playing in my head.

He pulls out a chair and sits opposite me. "And how do you feel about that?"

"Who are you, my therapist?" I ask, pursing my lips.

"If that's what you need," he replies, the smart-ass, but then holds his hands up in retreat. "I'm just playing around. But I am here for you if you need to talk."

My eyes narrow. "Thank you, Atlas, but I'm okay. Rhett and I are friends now."

"Friends," he scoffs under his breath. "Do you really believe that? Bikers aren't friends with women they want. He'll just pretend to be your friend until he gets what he wants from you."

I pretend I didn't hear that last part. "Yes, because I don't want to hurt Cara. She and I are working on our relationship and I don't need anything to ruin that. What else did you hear?"

"Just that you accidentally slept with your sister's ex," he says, just as Bronte walks up, her mouth dropping open.

"Okay, I'd like to pretend like I didn't hear that comment, but I did. Say what now?" she asks, sitting down on the corner of my desk.

Sighing, I rest my head on my desk and then sit back up. "I met a biker, I liked the biker, so I slept with him. And then he took me to a party, and Cara was there, and it just so happens that said biker is her ex-boyfriend. And not just any ex, he's *the* ex. They grew up together, and were in love with each other for half of their lives."

Bronte's eyes widen. "Rhett? Are you talking about Rhett? So now what? How does one come back from this?"

"Well, I was pretending it didn't happen until Atlas over here brought it up," I reply in a dry tone.

Bronte slaps at his arm. "You're such a gossip."

"I just wanted to make sure she was okay," he says, shrugging. "The best way to deal with shit is to talk about it."

"Okay, let's talk about you then. Who are you fucking right now?" I ask him.

Bronte makes a choking noise, but Atlas simply smiles slowly, flashing me his straight white teeth. "The question is, who am I not fucking right now?" he replies with a straight face.

I roll my eyes. "No one here, that's for sure."

Bronte laughs under her breath. "Come to think of it, I've never seen you with a woman, Atlas. Where are you keeping them?"

"I'm a private man and I won't be showing any woman off until I've found the one I want to be my old lady," he declares sincerely. "So when the time comes that you do see me with a woman, know that she's going to be mine."

Okay, his little speech is kind of hot, and from Bronte's wide-eyed look, she must have thought so, too.

Aries walks over and speaks to his brother. "Temper just called. He needs us."

Atlas quickly stands. "Tell Cam the boss called. Diesel is still here out back."

"I will," Bronte replies, and the two of them disappear. "They are so different."

"Tell me about it. Aries is so quiet, and Atlas never shuts up."

Bronte smirks. "I know. So you have a thing for bikers too, huh?"

My lip twitches. "I guess so."

She comes over and wraps her arm around my shoulders. "It will be okay. You'll end up with whoever you're meant to be with. And there happen to be a lot of bikers around here, in case you didn't notice."

Yeah, but none of them are Rhett.

And I didn't go looking for a biker; I just happened to fall for one.

Sighing, I look up at the roof of my house later that day, and then at the bucket on the floor which is half filled with water. "Yeah, that is going to be expensive," I mutter.

Cara had come over after I returned from work. She looks down at the bucket. "I can ask Decker to get up on the roof and take a look; he's pretty handy."

I know that Rhett would take care of it if I mentioned it to him, but I don't want to bother him. He's confided in me that things with the transition to president are not as easy as he thought and he's been stressed. One thing I love is how open he is about what he is going through and struggling with. I don't dare let myself wonder, or ask, how he is relieving stress because we're just friends.

"That would be nice," I reply after hesitating. "Only if he doesn't mind. There's obviously a hole in the roof somewhere, just what I need."

"You sure you don't want to sell this house, Con? It needs a lot of maintenance, which is expensive," she comments, frowning at the ceiling.

"I know," I admit. "Maybe you're right. Actually, I know you're right. The debts just keep adding up every time I have to fix something."

"But you're emotionally attached to it?"

"Something like that," I mutter. "I know how dumb it sounds. I didn't even have the best childhood here. But I guess it's all that I've ever known."

"Change can be good sometimes," she points out.

She's right.

And maybe it's time some change headed my way.

Chapter Sixteen

Rhett

I park my car across the road, keeping my sunglasses and hat on so hopefully no one will notice me, my eyes on the house.

"What are we doing here again?" Dice asks me quietly. When I told him I needed him as backup, he got into my car, no questions asked, and I appreciate the loyalty.

"Yesterday I saw a car following me," I admit. "I wrote down the plate number and traced it back to this house. I mean, it could have been stolen. It's registered under a woman's name. I don't know, the whole thing is a little sketchy."

After the whole fiasco with Marko, the Forgotten Children gang leader who wanted me dead, I'm a little on edge. A few months ago I had accidentally shot his son when a gunfight broke out, and Marko was out for blood. I didn't know the kid was there. They had started the fight, and we were just defending ourselves. The whole thing was messed up, and I was really upset that it happened. If I had known they had a kid with them, I would have just retreated. I still have nightmares about that night.

After that the Wind Dragons sent me away until the heat died down, but instead Marko went after Cara, knowing that she meant something to me. The whole thing was a big mess.

Decker stepped in and protected Cara while I was hiding away, and they fell in love. Everyone told me Cara was safe, but it should have been me protecting her. Just another time I chose myself over Cara. I'm embarrassed to even think about it. Con also got caught in the cross fire. I didn't know who she was or what was going on, but I found out later she was targeted, too.

"Someone is coming out now," Dice murmurs, pulling me from my thoughts.

An attractive blonde woman comes out of the house and gets into her car. It must be Lacey Jones, the lady the car is registered to. I've never seen her before, though, and I have no idea why she'd be following me. She looks innocent enough, kind of like a librarian. But I know better than to judge a woman by her appearance. No one would think Clover or Cara are both trained well enough to snap a man's neck in an instant either.

"She's cute," Dice comments, a smirk playing on his lips. "Is she one of the ways you've been getting over Con?"

My lips tighten. "I've never seen this woman before. Also, shut the hell up about Con."

"Come on, can you blame me? Leah told me about Con and how you never even cheated on Cara. That's complicated shit, man."

My eyes narrow. "So much for client confidentiality."

"I understand why you did it, you know. There's been so many times when I've thought to myself that Leah could do much better than me—she could be with some other intellect with a degree and a normal job—so I get it," he comments, surprising me. "But I'm too selfish to let her go, so props to you for not being selfish."

"I think I was being selfish and now I have to try not to be."

"What do you mean? You wanted what was best for Cara, so you did what you had to so she could have the life she wanted and deserved."

I give him a look. "You're telling me that Leah would be fine if you made decisions about your relationship for her without even talking to her about it?"

Dice cringes. "Well, when you put it like that, yeah, you're a dumb fuck, man."

I laugh at his honesty. "You're right, but I don't know, with how things are going now, I think it's just what was meant to happen with us. It was just our time to part. She never wanted to be with a biker, never mind a president. We grew up watching relationships like that and we all saw firsthand how much the women have to sacrifice. Not to mention the danger that they are put in every day. The stories I could tell you… The clubhouse was a little different back in the day."

"How so?" he asks, sounding interested.

"Everyone was there more—the men basically lived there and so did the women. It was like one big family, and the second my mom became involved with Talon, I was included in that family, just like that," I explain, smiling at the memories. "The MC had such loyalty for each other, and all the OGs were in their prime. I want that for us. It's our turn now."

"You'll make it so, Rhett. I believe in you," Dice replies, looking out the window. "We all do."

"Do you think the new members have that dedication and loyalty to the club? To making us a family? I can't make anything happen unless we have people around who want the same."

Dice studies me. "I don't know, man. I don't think we've seen everyone's true colors yet. It would take some time before we see who the men really are."

I nod. "I agree."

I have to wonder if this is why Arrow is stepping down now. This new generation is so different from theirs. It's like these guys are just in the MC to get laid, and I learned early on that it's more than that.

We go silent for a few seconds, until Dice breaks it. "Now what? Should we break into her house and see if we can find anything?"

I smirk at his suggestion. "No, not just yet. I'll come back if I need to. We better head back."

The MC decided just today that we will have a boxing tournament where basically we're all versus each other and fight until there's one last man standing. After learning that Decker is a better-trained fighter than me, I've been wanting to step up my game, because my pride took a little hit. The fiasco with Marko ended in a match between his best fighter and me. Decker had to step in for me when I was pretty much going to get killed. So yeah, not going to let that happen again.

I'm not used to anyone being better than me at shit, and I don't like it. Not that I'd ever admit this out loud.

When we pull up at the clubhouse and get out of the car, Sledge is standing out the front talking to Zeke and Bear, another two of our just-patched-in members. These are the men that I will grow with, just like Arrow has with my dad, Rake, Tracker, Wolf, Sin, Irish and the rest of the original Wind Dragons members. They have all stood by each other through thick and thin: prison, deaths, attacks, crime, breakups, pregnancies… everything.

And I want my generation to have that same loyalty to each other.

"Who is fighting first?" Dice asks, studying Sledge's huge size in apprehension.

I laugh at his expression. "Yeah, let's put Sledge last."

"What shady shit have you two been up to?" Bear asks, running his hand through his black hair. His hazel eyes are almost otherworldly, swirls of brown and green.

"Shady?" Dice asks, closing my car door.

"You took the car instead of your bikes. Dead give-away." Bear smirks, ducking as Zeke playfully punches him.

"Nothing too shady, just a little stakeout."

"You ready for this tournament?" Sledge asks, the bastard knowing he has it over us in size. However, you know what they say: the bigger the man, the harder the fall. He might be massive, but he won't be as fast as the rest of us.

"I'm ready."

"What does the winner get?" Zeke asks. "Besides bragging rights."

"Let's fight for Leah," Bear comments, then runs as

Dice starts going after him. He's going to regret that comment when he steps into the ring.

We put Zeke against Dice first, and the fight gets bloody pretty soon, but neither of them wants to give up. Zeke ends up winning with one last punch to Dice's stomach, which has him dropping to his knees.

I beat Bear, but not without working for it, and then I take on Zeke. We all fight each other in knockout rounds until it comes to me and Sledge, and I can't help but have flashbacks to when I had to fight Stalk, one of Marko's henchmen, a man who is even bigger and wider than Sledge.

I lost that one, but I'm not going to lose now.

Sledge swings his large fist out at me and I duck, get back up and hit him right in the gut. His knee comes up and I move back just in time, another punch narrowly missing the side of my head. We keep going like this, and I can see he's getting tired, his movements becoming slower. Eventually I kick him in the stomach, then punch him in the head, and he goes down.

The men all clap, and I see Arrow leaning against the wall, watching us.

I don't know when he's going to step down and hand the MC over to me. Whenever he thinks I'm ready, I guess. I know I went off track with the Cara breakup, but now I'm moving forward from that and on with my life.

I haven't spoken to Con since I left her house last weekend, and I think it's for the best. I haven't slept with anyone since her, which has been unlike me as of recent. I haven't even got drunk. While the men have been giving me a little bit of shit about it, the lack of distractions is allowing me to concentrate on what's most important—the Wind Dragons MC.

"My turn," Sin calls out as he steps into the ring. He beckons Tracker forward with his hand. "Brother? Just like the old days."

Tracker laughs and joins him. "All right. But Lana is going to kill you if you mess up my face."

"Better duck fast then."

The two of them play around, and we all watch, laughing at their antics.

This is our brotherhood, the brotherhood, and I'm not going to let anything stand in the way of it.

Chapter Seventeen

Con

"Are you all right?" Cara asks, brow furrowing as she touches my forehead. "Your temperature is fine."

"Yeah, I just feel a little dizzy," I reply, sitting back down on my bed and staring at the TV.

"I'll get you some Tylenol," she murmurs, heading to the kitchen to get some out of her handbag.

We went out for lunch where we discussed me looking at potentially selling the house, and then came back to my place to watch a movie and eat the cheesecake we bought on the way home. It's been good, but also a little awkward at times. We haven't mentioned Rhett once, and although it's nice to pretend that never happened I think it's also something we should be having another proper discussion about. However, I know she probably thinks she's doing me a favor by not bringing it up. Decker came over yesterday and had a look at my roof, and was luckily able to fix the leak. So I got lucky for now, but it's only a matter of time until the next thing falls apart.

She comes back to bed and hands me two little white

tablets, and I swallow them with some of the water on my bedside table. "Thank you."

To be honest I haven't been feeling great all morning, and I have no idea what it is. I hope I'm not getting sick, because I don't want to miss any days of work.

"I'm glad we stopped at that dessert place, because this cookies-and-cream cheesecake is amazing," she says, smiling over at me. "You sure you're okay?"

I nod. "Yeah, I just hope I'm not getting sick. And I agree. I'm definitely going to be going back for more."

We sit silently for a while, eating our cheesecake.

"Do you want to talk about Rhett?" she suddenly asks, brow furrowing. "I know he is the elephant in the room here, but I wasn't sure if you wanted to."

"I think we should," I agree, nodding. "I don't want him to ever come between us."

"He won't," she promises. "I just wanted to say that you don't have anything to feel guilty about. It's not the best situation, but it's in the past. I don't want things to be weird between us."

"Do you think he liked me because I look like you?" I blurt out, asking the question that has been nagging me since I first found out who he was.

Her eyes widen, and she tilts her head, considering my words. "I honestly don't think that would be why. You're a gorgeous girl, Con, and we do have a few similarities, but it's not like we're twins. You are your own person, and I don't blame him for liking you. You're beautiful, and down-to-earth, and honest. And I don't want to stand in the way of you and him."

"Cara, I could never be with him knowing that he was your first love. It would be even more awkward, and even though you are saying it's okay, deep down I would always wonder if it was. I don't know, the whole thing doesn't sit right with me."

She puts her plate of cheesecake down and turns to face me, grabbing my hands in hers. "Con. I have moved on. Rhett and I will never be anything more than friends who used to date. I've made peace with that and he has, too."

That's news to me. "You don't know that. He'll always love you…"

"Yes, and I'll always love him. But we realized we haven't been *in* love in a long time."

"Have you two talked?"

She nods. "And I take it you two haven't, really."

I shake my head no. We have talked, but not about Cara. Not really.

"I think you should. There is a lot he should tell you and I'll let him do that on his own time. Once you do, you can decide if you want to be with him. And if you do, then be with him. I shouldn't be a part of whether you two date or not. I don't want that on me," she says quietly. "Just think about that. And you can always be honest with me about anything."

I nod. "Thank you for bringing it up. I feel better talking about it and not just pretending that nothing happened."

Because boy, did it happen.

"Me too," she agrees.

"Rhett and I decided to just be friends," I let her know. Even though we slept together. That was just a onetime setback, right?

She seems to find that amusing. "Okay, let me know how that goes."

We finish the movie and then she heads home, telling me to call her if I need anything. When she leaves I find myself in the bathroom, feeling nauseous. I must be getting a tummy bug, and I just hope I didn't give it to Cara, too.

When I wake up the next morning I'm still not feeling great, so I call in sick at work and spend the day in bed, eating crackers and drinking ginger ale. I'm feeling much better by the afternoon, so I get some cleaning done around the house.

The next morning, I feel nauseous again, and a terrifying thought enters my mind. I get in my car and drive to the pharmacy to pick up a pregnancy test. I've been feeling nauseous every morning for three days now, and it's not going away. I couldn't be pregnant, though, could I? I realize that my period is a little late, but it's not unusual for me to go a few days over. I decide to take the test just so I can relax instead of overthinking.

When I get home, I sit down on the toilet and pee on the stick. I place it on the sink while I wash my hands and then pace around the bathroom.

I'm overwhelmed right now. I don't think I've ever been this scared in my life. I haven't slept with anyone except Rhett in the last few months, so if I'm pregnant, the child is his.

Nothing like a pregnancy scare with a man you don't think you can be with to really throw a wrench in the works.

"Please don't be pregnant," I whisper to myself, squeezing my eyes shut and taking a few deep breaths.

Please.

This is not what I need right now, and it would be the worst timing in the world.

Please.

After a few moments I finally force myself to look down at it.

Two little blue lines.

Happiness for others, devastation for me.

Under any other circumstance this moment would probably be happiness for me, too. If I were pregnant by any other man, this probably would have been a shock, but I would have adapted and been happy.

I don't know how I'm going to adjust to having my sister's ex-boyfriend's firstborn child.

Fuck.

What a mess.

What am I going to do?

Cara might be okay with Rhett and I being together, but everyone else will sure have a problem with it. And now that I'm pregnant? People will probably think I trapped him. I'm about to drop this bombshell on everyone and I'm going to look like I planned all of this.

I go back to bed and cry, knowing that shit is about to get a whole lot worse before it gets better.

If it ever does get better.

I head to work the next day, in denial, and pretend like everything is fine. I haven't told anyone that I'm pregnant, and I don't know when I will. I bring some ginger ale and crackers to work to get me through my awful morning sickness, and luckily for me I manage to hide it well enough. I find Atlas in the storeroom unpacking the new stock.

"Want some help?" I ask. The morning has been slow, and Bronte is out front helping customers who want to buy some merchandise.

Atlas raises his brow, and looks down at the heavy box in his hands. "Do I want you to help me carry shit? That would be a firm no."

I roll my eyes. "You're such a caveman. I can help put the stuff on the shelves, you can do the heavy lifting."

Normally, I would just carry the boxes too, but I guess I shouldn't be doing those things anymore. My whole life is going to change in more ways than one. At least I have a better job now to provide for a child.

I freeze. Wait, does that mean I've decided that I'm definitely going to have this child?

I love Cara, but not enough not to keep my baby, no matter who the father is.

Is that selfish of me?

With this one, I need to follow my heart, because I'm the one who is going to have to live with the consequences of my decision for the rest of my life, no one else.

"You okay?" Atlas asks, box still in his hands. "You look a little pale."

"I'm fine, just recovering from being sick over the weekend," I lie.

He nods apologetically. "How much did you drink?"

I go along with his presumption. "Too much."

"No wonder you brought some soda and crackers in with you." The man misses nothing. "I can head out and grab you something if you need it, just let me know," he offers.

"Thanks, Atlas, that's very sweet of you, but I think I'll be okay," I reply, smiling at him.

I manage to get through the rest of the workday without too much suffering, but it starts up again when I get home and am left alone with my thoughts.

I'm going to have to tell Rhett.

Do I tell him now, or do I wait three months until I'm at a safe stage in the pregnancy? Is that selfish of me?

Probably. But it would be awful if I upset everyone and then something went wrong and I had a miscarriage.

I don't know what the right answer is, but I do have time to think it over and make the best choice. I'm just going to have to brace myself for Cara's reaction. This child is going to be her niece or nephew, and I know she loves Rhett, so once she gets over the shock, maybe she will accept my child with open arms.

At the end of the day, she's a good person and I need to have faith in that.

Why didn't we use a condom? I have a contraceptive implant, but of course that is just my luck. I need to make an appointment with my doctor to discuss that, and the pregnancy.

And as for Rhett? I've avoided him the last few days. I've never been gladder that he's busy with the MC and lives a few hours away.

Little does he know, shit is about to hit the fan.

Chapter Eighteen

Rhett

Over the next week, I can tell something is brewing. Arrow has been spending a lot of time with me talking out various parts of our businesses. I've been focused and undistracted. While they have slowly been showing me the ropes for some time now, they are definitely amping it up.

I spend the day being shown all the MC accounts, how it all works and where the money comes from and where it goes. Arrow and I discuss all our business ventures, and I know it's up to me to maintain all this money coming in, and to make good choices to ensure all the members get paid enough. As of now, we are all doing really well financially, and I know that's because of how Sin and Arrow have set up the business side for our club. Right now I get more money than I ever would in a nine-to-five job, and I'd like to keep it that way.

"Not all fun, is it?" Arrow comments, amusement dancing in his eyes. "That's what we have a treasurer for, though, so you can get them to handle most of this shit. You just have to know what's happening, and make sure you're on top of it all."

"It might not be fun, but money is fun, so I'm okay with it." I grin, sitting down at the big wooden table where we hold all of our meetings, eyeing the president's chair at the head. "I actually like learning about all of this, and how we make our income. It's like the best of both worlds—I get to be a biker, but also start and maintain businesses, juggle stocks and investments. Maybe I should wear a suit to the clubhouse sometimes."

Arrow smirks. "You were born for this, you know that? When Nate was born I thought maybe he would take over one day, but early on I knew he didn't want to. This wasn't the life for him; he wanted to stretch his wings and follow his own path. We all had our eyes on you, but didn't want to put any pressure on you."

"This is where I'm meant to be." I nod.

And now I have nothing holding me back. Cara was right. In the long run us breaking up was the right choice, and she deserves a life that she wants. The moment of realization is a good one. I now get to be who I want to be, lead the MC and put the Wind Dragons first, no matter what. She still falls under that jurisdiction, and I will always be here to protect her and all the MC families. Clover, Con…everyone.

Con.

I had a dream about her last night and woke up hard as a rock. I took care of it myself, which also isn't usually like me; I'd generally have someone look after that. But since we've been… I don't even know what we're doing.

She's under my skin and I can't seem to shake her. She asks nothing of me and never questions anything. She isn't clingy or making demands. She must be playing mind tricks 'cause it's making me want her even more. I might block her from my thoughts during the day, but now she's finding me at night when I'm vulnerable and have no control over my thoughts. I've decided to give us some space. I need to really focus on the MC and get that situated before I pay any attention to my social life.

I both love it and hate it.

"Do you still have your eyes on Marko?" I ask Arrow, sitting down at the table.

"I called them off. Why?" he asks, frowning.

"Just asking. I thought I saw someone following me the other day, which led me to a woman's house. I thought maybe it had something to do with Marko, because I can't think of any other reason someone would be following me."

Arrow barks out a deep laugh and slaps me on the shoulder. "It could be Marko, but it could be anyone. Always assume you have a target on you, Rhett. Trust no one. We have that dirt on Marko, and if he pulls any shit we will be using it. Then the FC won't want him as their leader anymore. I knew we should have killed that bastard."

He's talking about the fact that Marko is a confidential informant for the FBI. When the fight ended and Decker won, we had one last card to play. We told Marko that if he messed with any one of us, or the Knights of Fury MC, who helped us get this informa-

tion, we'd tell his men all about his extracurriculars
with the Feds. He's been in line ever since.

"Yeah, but none of us want to do time," I reply in a
dry tone, tilting my head and looking up at him. "Unless we really have to."

It's likely at some stage in my life I will have to
spend time behind bars. I know it, Arrow knows it. We
all know it. That wall of mug shots didn't come about
as a coincidence.

And I'll do what I need to do to protect those that
I love.

"Well, it's the only reason he's still standing, but if
we need to take care of him, we will. There are a few
buyers interested in the Toxic strip clubs. What do you
think about selling them?"

"How much are they making us right now?" I ask.
We have three different Toxic locations, but I don't
know the exact amount these venues are bringing in
for us. After all, the strippers keep their own money,
so what we get comes from the bar and entrance fees.

He slides me a folder, and when I open it, my jaw
drops. "Uh, yeah. I think we will be keeping them.
Damn, horny men must have bottomless wallets."

Arrow nods. "It's good for the women, too. They
know we will keep them safe, and we don't charge them
anything to dance, whereas other places do. No one
messes with them, because the customers know we own
the joint."

I never thought of it that way, but he's right. The
women there do have it pretty good, and we would
never let anyone harm or disrespect them. They are all
walked to their cars at nighttime, and we do anything

we can to ensure their safety. Basically, we aren't ass-holes to them.

"All right, Toxic stays," I murmur.

It's good business for the club. The MC got out of dealing drugs a while back, and that's something I'm going to stick to. The members are probably wondering where I'm going to lead the club, but it's not going to be backward. Since Sin took the reins, before Arrow, we've tried to stay on the right side of the law when it comes to our businesses. Sure, we have weapons and guns at the clubhouse that may not have permits, but that's as far outside the law Arrow has let it get, except in extreme cases when we are protecting ourselves. If we go to jail, it's not going to be for something stupid like drugs or illegal business deals.

"You've made this job easy for me," I say, grinning. "You know that? The businesses are running, the money is coming in, the men are all good men and everyone is happy."

Arrow's lip twitches. "When you're the one every-one runs to when something goes wrong? You'll realize it's not easy. Men betray you, even members. Business deals fall through and people double-cross you. You'll be the one making all the final decisions and keeping everyone together. When you fail, everyone does. When you win, everyone does. It's a lot of pressure."

Just when I was feeling good about it.

"I want the club to be like it always was. Like you guys had it when I was growing up."

Arrow goes silent for a few seconds before speaking. "It will never be the same, Rhett. The world changes. This generation is different from the one I grew up in.

I don't think you should try to replicate how it was. Just make it the best you can."

He's right.

I can't make the clubhouse exactly like it was, because the same people won't be there, and that's what made it.

But I can make it the best I can.

"I will definitely try."

"People will test you when I step down, to see what you're made of," he continues, running his fingers through his brown-and-gray beard. "And you need to show them who you are. That you aren't to be messed with. We're all still here to guide you. I'm still here. You'll be fine."

"How long until I turn into a cynical bastard like you?"

He laughs again. "Give it a few years. I have faith in you, though. You are a lot more carefree than I ever was."

I don't feel carefree, but I like that he sees me that way.

I guess only time will tell.

We all head out together as an MC for a ride, visiting one of the other MC chapters. When we're done, instead of returning to the clubhouse I ride the two hours to my new pad, passing Con's house on the way.

Her lights are on, but I don't stop by.

Chapter Nineteen

Con

I hear the rumbling of a motorcycle passing my house and sigh. After seeing my doctor on my lunch break today, who confirmed that I am indeed four weeks pregnant, I had to go back to work and pretend like everything was okay. It was hard. I'm really emotional, and I know it's probably because of my hormones, but I feel pretty weak and tired and confused. I need to speak to someone but I don't know who I can turn to. Jamie, maybe.

But she's not who I really want to tell, is she?

I type out a text to Rhett, but then delete it.

It's a real shit show of a situation. If I tell him, it's going to blow up, but if I don't tell him, when he does find out it will blow up, too. I can't win. I think I just need to be honest about everything.

But not over text.

This definitely has to be a face-to-face, in-person conversation.

And after I tell Rhett, then I will tell Cara.

Pray for me.

The nausea isn't so bad at work the next day, and I push everything aside and concentrate on my tasks for the day. Two men come in to pick up their motorcycles, and I take their payments after Cam speaks to them. I can tell that they are both extremely happy with her work, and who wouldn't be?

After work I grab some Chinese takeout and head home. I haven't thought about the house since Decker fixed the roof, and I know I need to get my ass in gear to figure everything out. I open the door of one of my spare rooms and look around. There's nothing in here, just an empty space.

I touch my stomach and look down at it. "It might just be me and you. I hope you're going to be okay with that."

I mean, we might not have a choice.

Later that night, Rhett comes by and just gives me a huge hug. We don't even have sex, he just falls asleep with his head on my stomach. If only he knew what was in there.

I didn't even get to tell him that I'm pregnant.

Maybe it's a sign. Maybe I should wait a few more weeks and tell him then. After all, it is really early days. And then I realize that is just fear talking. I know I need to tell him.

I spend the rest of my weekend cleaning and sorting out my house, and checking my damn phone, waiting to see if Rhett actually ever replies. By Monday morning, he still hasn't, so I push any thoughts of him to the side and get on with my week, promising myself that if I do not hear from him by Friday, I'll ask him to come talk.

Well, at least I try.

"How are you this morning?" Cam asks when I arrive at work.

"I'm good, how are you?" I ask. I really like all the staff here, and I want to get to know them all better. It's a little intimidating when they are such a close group, but I hope I can be a part of that as time goes on.

"Can't complain. The sun is out. My man is fine as hell. Our wait list has grown even longer," she replies with a bright smile, her perfectly lined pink lips kicking up at the corners.

I laugh. I needed that. Orion *is* pretty fine, if you like that businessman type of guy. "Of course the wait list has grown. You're extremely talented," I say, sitting down at my desk and getting everything ready for the morning.

"Thank you." She beams. "I really like having you here, Con. I'm glad that we hired you."

"Me too," I reply, emotion hitting me. It's so nice to feel appreciated, and it just makes me want to work even harder. I wish more employers realized this.

On my lunch break I go to our local café and order coffee and a croissant, then sit down by myself at a table. I know many people don't like eating alone, but I don't mind it, and I never have. I'm perfectly comfortable with my own company, probably because I grew up thinking I was an only child.

"Hey there," a good-looking gentleman says, sitting at the table next to me. He looks to be in his midthirties, and is well-groomed with dark hair and eyes. His suit leads me to assume he's a professional.

"Hello," I reply, arching my brow.

"This is my first time here. Anything I should try?" he asks, scanning the menu.

"And how do you know it's not my first time here?" I reply, taking a sip of my coffee.

"I'm just guessing. You look pretty comfortable in your surroundings."

"I could just be a very confident woman." I grin. "And to be honest, everything here is pretty good, especially the waffles and the berry cheesecake. Although today, my pregnant self is eying a pickle sandwich, so I probably can't be trusted."

His eyes widen for a second.

"Noted," he replies, smiling. "Thanks. I'm Marvin, by the way."

"Constance."

He offers his hand and I shake it. "Lovely to meet you."

"You too," I reply.

He gets up and goes over to the counter to order, and I finish off my food and then head back to work. When I'm on my way home at the end of the day, I swear that I see the same man driving past me in his car, but I can't be sure.

Weird.

Jamie calls me to tell me that things with her fiancé are a little rocky at the moment.

"Shouldn't you guys still be in the honeymoon phase?" I ask, trying not to sound negative, but also trying to be the voice of reason. I haven't even met this guy yet, but I don't get the best vibes from him.

"Yeah, we should," she agrees. "But I don't know,

he's just so hot and cold. I don't know what to think. Maybe he's having second thoughts about the wedding."

"You should just talk to him," I suggest. "And I still have to meet him. We should organize a dinner or something."

"Sounds good," she replies. "And yeah, okay, I'll try to talk to him and see where his head is at. I really want this to work, Con. I know it sounds crazy, but I love him. He's the one for me, I know it. He spoils me so much. You should hear the trip he has planned for our honeymoon."

"Okay, well, let me know how it goes."

We end the call and I think about the fact that I never tell anyone about my personal problems or issues going on in my life. Jamie knows a little about Rhett, but not the full story, and no one knows that I'm pregnant. My mother always told me that I was closed off and never showed much emotion, but I'm pretty sure that it was a trauma response from her and Dad's parenting, or lack thereof. I was kind of left to fend for myself most of the time, and I've learned to only rely on me, myself and I.

Rhett finally texts me back.

Rhett: Sorry about the other night, passing out on you and then leaving first thing. The club needed me—I had to ride back. Everything okay? What do you want to talk about?

Con: Can you let me know when you are back here next?

Rhett: Sure thing.

I leave it at that. I want to speak to him face-to-face—there's no point going back and forth in text.

I enjoy the calm before the storm. Right now, this is as peaceful as it's going to get for me, and I'm going to appreciate it while I can.

Because when the truth comes out?

My world as I know it is going to change.

"That Way" by Tate McRae plays in the car on my way to work, and after I park I sit there and listen until it finishes. I feel the heartfelt lyrics in the song, I really do.

When I get into the garage, Temper is there, which is a rare occasion. He usually has everyone else running around for him. I guess it's the perks of being the owner and having a whole staff and motorcycle club at his disposal. Cam is showing him some designs, and Atlas is sitting at Bronte's desk, going through her snack drawer and stealing some of her chocolate.

"It's not even nine a.m. and you're already stealing her treats," I say.

He grins. "I brought you coffee. It's on your desk."

"Thank you," I reply, perking up. I head to my desk and leave him to his business. Temper comes over and says hello and goodbye and then leaves.

"Everything okay?" I ask Cam as I drink my coffee. I then realize that I probably shouldn't drink coffee anymore and put the delicious drink down unhappily.

She nods. "Yeah, we are just upping the security here. We always upgrade with whatever new technology comes out. So Temper was checking out the cameras and alarms. He seems to be a little on alert, though, so maybe something is going on." She shrugs it off like it's no big deal. "Orion is coming in today to pick up his latest bike. I swear he's my biggest customer."

I smile. "That's pretty damn cute."

She beams. "I know. He brings us in a lot of business."

"Do you know what's going on?" I ask Atlas as he walks past.

"With what?" he asks, expression giving nothing away.

"Do you guys have shit going on with the MC?"

Atlas studies me and then laughs. "If we did, we wouldn't be going around telling people about it. Unless you are a member of the MC, you don't need to know."

Huh.

Intrigued, I decide to ask him a few more questions about motorcycle clubs, so I can understand exactly what Rhett's life is like. "Can women be members?"

He shakes his head. "Not officially, no. Why? You want to join?"

Smirking with amusement, I roll my eyes. "No, I'm just curious. I do want to learn how to ride a motorcycle, though. Would you teach me?"

Atlas looks at me like I've grown a second head. "Sure, if you want to start a MC war."

"What do you mean?" I ask, confused. How would that start a war?

"Did Rhett take you on the back of his bike?" he asks, studying me a little too closely.

"Yeah, why?"

"Then you're his," he replies with a shrug. "I'm not getting involved in that shit, no offense. I took Nadia on the back of my bike once, and I still have to watch my back around Trade."

I blink slowly. "So you're telling me only their women can go on the back of their bikes?"

"Yeah, and although you and Rhett aren't together, there's obviously some shit going on there, so I think you should ask him to teach you. Which, by the way, is sexy as fuck," he comments, grinning. "Rhett is going to take over the Wind Dragons one day soon, everyone knows it, so I don't need to piss him off for no good reason."

"I see," I murmur. I don't quite know what he means by "take over" the Wind Dragons, but I guess I should ask Rhett. "Well, Rhett and I are just friends, so I'm definitely not his. But I can understand you not wanting to get involved in the mess that is my life. Maybe I'll just go to a riding school."

"You could ask Clover," he suggests. "I've heard she's been riding before she could even drive."

I nod, even though I know I'm not going to. I don't want to ask Clover for anything, especially when we are finally on decent terms. I don't want to push it. We definitely aren't close enough for me to ask her for favors. I would ask Cara, but I've kind of been avoiding her ever since I found out I'm pregnant. Maybe it's a way of self-preservation for me, knowing that soon she's probably going to be really upset with me, so I'm pulling away to save myself some of the pain that I know is coming my way very soon.

Thinking of the baby reminds me that I won't be riding anything for the next eight months, so the motorcycle thing is going to have to wait anyway.

That thought puts me in a solemn mood, but then I think about the child I'm growing inside of me and I know that any sacrifices I have to make will be well worth it. I find myself daydreaming at work, wondering what he or she will look like, and thinking about names I love.

By the time I'm on my way home I'm exhausted, probably because I didn't sleep much last night. To say I'm more than a little surprised that I see Rhett when I get home is an understatement. He's standing next to his bike, looking down at his phone when I pull up in my car.

"What are you doing here?" I ask. I mean, I know I told him I wanted to speak to him about something, but I didn't think he'd be here so quickly, and without any notice.

He opens my car door and waits for me to get out. "You said you wanted to talk, so I'm here."

I arch my brow. "You mean the MC sent you here to do something for the club so you decided to stop in here, too?"

He opens his mouth, then closes it. "I'm in town on club business as well but—"

"I thought as much," I say, but I'm not really bothered by it. The fact that he came here the same day I told him I wanted to talk means something. He didn't have to stop by.

I walk to my front door. He follows behind me. I wasn't prepared to have to tell him so soon. I don't know how to say it.

Well, here goes nothing.

Chapter Twenty

Rhett

"Can I get you something to drink?" Con asks.

I shake my head. "No thank you."

I wasn't going to stop by, but the truth is, Arrow asked Dice to come here to handle some club business, but I offered to go instead. Mainly because I know Con wanted to talk about something, and because I didn't even reply to her text the other night when Arrow needed me at the clubhouse.

There were some territory issues with another MC, and Sledge ended up getting into a fight with a member of the Cursed Ravens MC named Shovel. I had to go in for some damage control, and to stop an MC war from breaking out, which is the last thing we need right now. We've never had issues with the Cursed Ravens before, and I don't want to start something just when shit's getting peaceful around here. I spoke with Gage, their president, and cleared the matter up. I know normally Arrow would handle this, but now he's letting me step in, probably to see what I'm made of. He's testing me, and I want to pass with flying colors.

I give my full attention to Con, waiting for her to tell me whatever is on her mind. I'm guessing it's about our so-called friendship, or me continuously dropping by to her house whenever I feel like it. We probably should define what we are. I know what we would be if it were solely up to me. The sex is out of this world and I can't seem to get enough of her.

But beyond that, she brings me peace. And comfort. I realize why it's necessary to have an old lady when you're president. Behind every member of an MC is the woman who holds him up. If my mother taught me anything, it's that a man doesn't need a woman and a woman doesn't need a man. But together they can be a powerful force. That's what Con is for me. I probably should make this official; I don't know what I'm waiting for.

"Okay," she whispers, more to herself than me, I think. "So basically I just wanted to tell you that—"

My phone starts to ring, and when I see Arrow's name pop up I know I have to answer it. "One second, sorry."

She nods, and distracts herself in the kitchen while I take the call.

"Yeah?"

"We need you at Toxic now. You're close by, right? There's a situation. One of the girls has been hurt."

"What?" I ask, concern and shock filling me. "I'm on my way."

How did this happen? We have every safety measure to make sure that it doesn't. I hope whoever it is, she's not too hurt.

"I'm so sorry, I have to go to Toxic," I say to Con,

looking up from my phone. "But hold that thought. I'll be back afterward."

I leave without her saying a word, jump on my bike and head to Toxic. When I get there, I find one of the dancers, Storm, sitting in the corner with an ice pack on her face.

"What happened?" I ask her, scowling. "Who did this?"

One of the security guards, Everett, steps forward. "She went to his car with him, and he attacked her."

I bring my eyes back to her. She starts to cry. "I'm sorry, he said he'd give me five thousand dollars if I... I know I shouldn't have. And I didn't do anything in the end. He just attacked me. I don't know why."

"It's okay," I tell her, gritting my teeth. "It's not your fault, Storm. You should never be treated this way—it's all on him. But we have these rules for a reason, and it's to keep you safe. If you leave the building, it makes it harder to do so. Do we have him on camera?"

Everett nods. "We have him coming in, and them two leaving."

He shows it to me on his phone. And it's a man I've personally never seen before, blond, tall and in his late twenties. "He's never to step in here again."

"Already on it."

"I'll find out who he is and teach him a lesson in how to treat women," I say, bending down and checking Storm's cheek. It looks like he punched her a few times in the face, the poor thing. "Do you want to go to the hospital?"

She shakes her head. "No, it will be okay. There's nothing they can do. I took some pain meds."

"Okay, go take a few days off. We'll give you some money so you don't have to worry," I assure her. "Stay out of trouble."

"I will. Thank you, Rhett."

I tell Everett to get her home safely, and then wonder why the fuck a man would tell her to come to his car and then attack her. It makes no sense.

I call Arrow and tell him it's sorted, and send him a picture of the man in question, and he replies to my text.

Arrow: Sending some men your way. Find him.

Let the hunt begin.

It's dark out when we find John, after one of the regulars tells us where he lives. No one protected him, which shows much about his character, not that we didn't already know that. My knuckles are covered in blood when we are finished, and I hope he learned his lesson to never lay hands on a woman again.

"A man paid me to do it," he'd said, which makes zero sense.

We all head back to the clubhouse, because it's too late for me to go to Con's now. She's going to be pissed. I send her a text, but I know what I did was messed up.

She's probably happy right now that we can never be together, because this is what life would be like as my woman. It's only going to get worse when I step in officially as president.

The thought that she might completely walk away from me hurts.

More than I thought it would.

I can see Con as my old lady, by my side, being my rock. That's where I picture us ending up, but if this is too much for her, I guess it's best to know now.

But I just fucking hope she sticks around for me.

Chapter Twenty-One

Con

When there's a knock at the door on Saturday morning, I sigh. I think this is the second or third time I've attempted to have this conversation with Rhett. Every time I get a chance to, something happens. I think this time I'm just going to blurt it out.

No warning.

No lube.

Just going in.

I test the words on my tongue. "I am pregnant."

Three words. I can say them.

How hard can it be?

I open the door. "I'm—"

I falter looking into his ocean eyes. Okay, pretty damn hard.

He waits patiently for me to speak, but when I say nothing he asks, "Are you okay?"

I nod. "Yes, of course. Come in."

"I'm sorry that I had to leave last night," he says as he gives me a kiss and then makes himself at home, sitting on the couch. "The club needed me. Although

I just drove all the way back here to see you, so I hope that gets me some brownie points." He wiggles his eyebrows.

I laugh, unable to control it despite the news I'm sitting on. He's a charmer. I sit down on the arm of my couch. "Yes, I figured."

"What did you want to talk about? It sounded important," he asks, studying me.

Well, here is the moment that I've been waiting for.

I shift nervously and tug on the hem of my T-shirt when I blurt out, "I'm pregnant. That's what I've been trying to tell you, and each time something happened, and…yeah. I'm pregnant."

There. I said it. I was honest with him. And now the ball is in his court.

Blue eyes widen, and he freezes. "You're…pregnant?"

I nod.

"And it's mine?" he asks, brow furrowing.

"I haven't been with anyone else, Rhett. Yes, it's yours. My contraception must not have worked, I don't know. I am as shocked as you are." I wring my hands, unsure what is going to happen next.

I study him, and watch every emotion pass on his expression. Surprise. Shock. Confusion. And then lastly, fear.

He looks down at my stomach, and then back up to my face. "I don't even know what to say. I'm going to need a minute. I'm sorry."

He walks out, and I sigh and close my eyes. I didn't know what reaction I was hoping for from him, but his wasn't the best. I mean, I suppose it wasn't the worst either, considering the situation. We aren't even together, we're just friends, and now we are bringing a baby into the world.

From here on out, what I want doesn't matter anymore. I have to make every decision with my unborn child's best interest at heart. I don't want to hurt Cara, but I can no longer put her feelings before mine. If Rhett wants to be a part of this child's life, then we'll be tied together, even if it isn't romantically.

Rhett comes back about a half an hour later, and I'm still frozen in the same spot.

He cups my nape, his palm gently dragging up to my cheek. "I'm sorry, I just needed to be alone to think. I... This is definitely a situation I didn't expect right now."

"Situation?" I repeat. My child is not a situation. "This *situation* can manage itself if you don't want to be a part of it. I don't need anything from you, Rhett."

"That's not what I meant—"

"I know this pregnancy is a huge surprise and you might not love the idea—"

"Con—"

"But this baby is coming, so while you're only getting your head around it, I need to protect it."

He sits down on the coffee table in front of me so we can see each other's faces properly.

"And if you don't want to have anything to do with us, I understand that, too. And there's no hard feelings," I continue.

"Do you truly believe that I'm the kind of man who would walk away from my child?" he asks, looking offended. "Yes, I need a little time to process this, but of course I'm going to be there as a father for my child. I'm a man, Con. I'm far from perfect, but I'd never walk away from my own flesh and blood. I don't know how some men do that, but that's not me."

Relief fills me. I wouldn't have held it against him if he wanted nothing to do with this, but I have to admit that I'm glad he's not walking away. "Okay. I'm sorry, I think I just needed to hear those words from you."

"I don't know how I'm going to manage the MC and a baby, but all the other men have done it, so I'm going to do it, too," he adds, taking a deep breath.

I nod. "It's not going to be easy."

"I know," he replies solemnly.

"And Cara—"

"Cara will be fine," he assures me. "I mean, it would be a shock to everyone. But…"

"There's not much else we can do right now," I conclude.

"Okay, I guess we are doing this then," he murmurs, the two of us staring into each other's eyes. I have no idea what this means for us, but I'm not going to think about that right now.

"Umm… I don't think we should be *together*. I mean, I know it'd be easier, but I also don't want the baby to be the reason we are together." Oh my God, shut up. Why is my mouth moving? "Not that you want to be with me. I mean, we're friends, right?" Kill me now.

He chuckles. "You're cute, you know that?"

I scrunch my face up. The last time a guy told me I was cute was when I was ten.

"I get what you're saying and I agree. I do like you and want to see where this goes, but I don't want that to be the reason either."

I feel oddly hopeful at his words. "I'll tell Cara next," I say, and he nods.

Then his phone rings, and he mutters a curse before answering it. "Hey? Yeah, okay." He ends the call and stands up. "I have to head back to the clubhouse. Do you need anything? I mean, can I do anything for you?"

I shake my head. "No, but thank you. I'm fine. You go and handle what you need do."

He bends down and kisses the top of my head, and then leaves.

I sink back into the couch and take a deep breath.

We're having a baby.

Chapter Twenty-Two

Rhett

Arrow couldn't have called at a worse time, but that just seems to be my luck. After I leave Con's house, my head still exploding from the bomb she dropped on me, I head back to the clubhouse, because Arrow is officially stepping down as president. I don't know if this was a planned date or a last-minute decision, but it's happening now whether I'm ready or not. Maybe he wanted to throw me into the deep end to see if I swim or drown.

I'm going to swim.

Today is the day. I'm going to be president of the Wind Dragons MC, the youngest one they've ever had, and it's also the day I find out that I'm going to be a father.

It's a lot to process, and I'm going to need time to get my head around it.

I couldn't think of a worse time than right now to have a baby.

My enemy list is going to grow, and the MC is going to consume all of my time. I don't know how I'm going to juggle both roles without neglecting one, or maybe

I'll have to half-ass both of them, which is something I don't want to do either.

I'm fucked.

I can't let the Wind Dragons down. I've been prepping for this moment for so long, but I don't want to let Con down either. Or my child. My biological father wasn't around to raise me, and I would never do that to Con or a child. I was lucky that Talon stepped in and took over that role, so I still had a father figure growing up.

And then there's Cara.

How's she going to take this news? And the rest of my family?

Probably better than I am.

Con said that she would tell Cara, so I'll leave that up to her and speak to Cara myself afterward. I have a feeling Cara is going to be fine with this. After our talk, I think that Cara is the least bothered by the idea of me and Con being together. But I have to wonder if this will hurt her.

This time when I step into the clubhouse, it feels different. This is *my* clubhouse now. My word is law, and it's up to me to lead the MC to do great things, and to protect each and every member and their families. All the victories and losses we have are now on my shoulders.

It's a lot of responsibility, I know.

But so is being a parent.

When I step into the room, every MC member is sitting around the large table, with Arrow in his usual spot at the head. He's holding his president patch in his hands, the one he has worn so proudly for so many years, now leaving his cut looking bare without it.

I walk over to him and he stands, shakes my hand and hands it to me.

After I take it, Arrow moves to the next chair, to my right, leaving me in the head seat.

This is a moment I'll never forget.

I sit down and look around the table at my brothers, my family. "Let's do this."

And with that everyone bangs on the table, cheering.

Chapter Twenty-Three

Con

With Rhett still at the clubhouse, I go to my first doctor's appointment alone. It's been a week since I told him, and he's been checking in with me every day, but he also just became president, so I assume he's busy right now. I don't really know much about being in an MC much less being a president of one. He did send me some flowers and Uber Eats yesterday, which was very sweet, along with a random chunk of money that appeared in my bank account.

At first I thought it was a mistake, but when I called the bank, they confirmed the deposit, and then Rhett asked if I'd received it. How did he even get my account number? I mean, don't get me wrong, not having to worry about money is nice, but I don't want him to feel like he's now obligated to look after me because I'm pregnant with his child.

I still haven't spoken to Cara; I've been putting it off and just enjoying no one else knowing for now, like a little secret just for me. I will tell her when I feel like the time is right.

An older blonde woman in a red coat sits next to me, glances my way and smiles. "The doctor is running late, so it looks like we're going to be here a long time."

"And that is why I asked for today off." I grin back.

"Me too," she laughs, and offers me her hand. "I'm Olivia."

"Con," I reply, shaking her hand.

Olivia starts to dig into her bag. "This nausea just won't let up. Do you want a cracker?"

"I'm okay, but thank you," I reply, watching as she nibbles on one. "How far along are you, if you don't mind me asking?"

"I'm about eight weeks now," she says. "And yourself?"

"I'm going to find out today for sure, but I'm thinking about six weeks," I say.

"Awesome, so we will be due around the same time. I live around here and am joining the local moms' group if you'd be interested."

"That actually sounds good." I have no idea what I'm doing, and some extra support would be great. We exchange numbers before I get called into the doctor's office, where I have my very first ultrasound. I send Rhett a photo and tell him that everything looks as it should.

Rhett: I'm so sorry I couldn't be there.

Con: It's okay, there will be plenty more.

Olivia sends me a text and the two of us start chatting about pregnancy. This is her second, so she knows more than I do. She tells me about her birth with her first child, and how easy it went until she had to start pushing, which took hours upon hours.

We talk about baby names. She loves the name Sloane, and I have no idea what names I like yet, because I picture having that conversation with Rhett first. It's nice having someone with no ties to Cara to talk to, someone who is just my friend and mine alone.

I have Jamie, and now I have Olivia.

It makes me feel like having this baby isn't going to be bad after all.

In fact, it's a blessing.

A month passes and so does most of the nausea, which makes being at work much easier. I still haven't told anyone else about being pregnant, not even Cara, and I find myself chatting with Olivia anytime I want to discuss something. We've been meeting for lunch and going to the mom group together, and she has fast become a big support in my life.

Rhett has been really busy settling in as president, but he has come and seen me every couple of days. Tonight he stopped by to take me out to dinner. We have been having date nights, but not sex, which is a bit confusing because I want him. But I know it's probably a bad idea to jump him every time I see him, especially now that we need to figure out how to be parents. Instead, we tell each other different stories about our lives or talk about what we think the baby will look like and what we picture our child to grow up like. It's been really nice.

"I hope our child has your chocolate-brown eyes,"

he says sweetly, tilting his head to the side. "Actually, I hope he or she looks exactly like you."

I grin. "Funny. I was thinking the exact same thing about you."

And that's when you know that you're having a child with the right person. I'd love for this baby to be just like Rhett. And no matter what happens between us, that opinion will never change.

Despite these sweet moments, it's a little tense being around him because we are avoiding the big elephant in the room—us as a couple—and just focusing on the baby. I think we're both being stubborn and neither of us wants to be the one to bring it up first.

"How long are we going to do this for?" he asks me finally.

"Do what?" I ask innocently, putting my fork down and giving him my full attention.

He absently watches the people around us, all enjoying their meals, before bringing his eyes back to me. "Pretend that we aren't together. You are the mother of my child, but that's not the reason I want to be with you. I wanted you before you were pregnant, you knew that, and I'll want you long after. Don't you want to be with me?"

Damn, does he have to call me out like this?

I lick my suddenly dry lips. "Of course I do. It's just not that simple, is it?"

"Con, have you talked to Cara about this?" he asks, scanning my eyes. "Or have you been avoiding talking about us and the baby like you've been avoiding talking to me?"

Damn. He knows me more than I give him credit for.

"I just… She's just…" I try to find the right words. "I can't betray her."

Rhett sits up and puts both elbows on the table, leaning toward me. "Talk to her. She might surprise you."

I nod. He's right. I can't keep this from her any longer, especially since I'm out of my first trimester and have no real excuse to keep it from her anymore.

"We can take it as slow as you want, but I want to try."

"I know, I want to try, too," I admit finally. "But until I talk with her we can't…"

His lip twitches. "Then you better tell her fucking soon."

The look he gives me is all heat, and I know he's right. The tension has built to peak level, and I want him badly.

But I know I've been avoiding telling Cara because I feel guilty. So yeah, I've been avoiding that shit and just being in my little bubble.

"Maybe we tell her together?"

My eyes snap to his at this declaration. *Together?* "Uh, I don't know if that is the best idea…"

"Con, look at me." He stares into my eyes and I can feel his conviction in just his gaze. "I've given you space. I've let you control what we are doing here. But Cara and I made peace a while ago. It's time for you and her to—"

"We did," I remind him. Although if I really think about it, we didn't really talk about my feelings for Rhett. I just kept telling her it wouldn't happen again.

Rhett just gives me a look. "Con, I think we can be something great, but we'll never know until we try."

"And then what?" I ask. "You're the president now; you aren't going to move here. And I'm just starting to love my life and job here. What are we going to do about the distance? Or are we just going to co-parent the best we can?" I don't want to leave my job, because I love it there, and Cara is over here, too. I guess I have some time before I have to worry about these things, but they are things I still have to think about in the near future.

"I would love you to move to the clubhouse, yes, but if you are completely against that, then we will make it work somehow."

I don't know what I want.

The next day Cara surprises me by dropping in with some wine and Chinese food.

"Hey," she says when I open the door, a genuine smile playing on her lips. "Are you busy? I feel like I haven't seen you in ages, so I thought I'd see if you wanted to hang out."

I open the door wider, excited, finally understanding what it means to be part of a family. A family that wants to hang out with you and cares about you. But then I realize I'm going to have to explain why I've been so detached. "Of course, come on in."

She puts the food and wine down on the coffee table and moves to my cabinets to grab silverware and plates. "Is everything okay with you, Con? You seem like you've been a little...distant. I told you I wasn't upset about Rhett, and I meant that."

It shows how much she cares that she has noticed that. "I know, and I'm sorry. To be honest, I've been wanting to talk to you, but I've kind of been putting it off, which is why I haven't seen you much."

She comes to sit down and starts taking the cartons out of the bag. "Well, I'm here now. What do you want to talk about?"

I clear my throat, clearly uncomfortable, so she continues. "Is this about Rhett? You know that if you and Rhett want to be together, I'm fine with it. Yes, it will be a little awkward for me at the start, but that's my problem, not yours. It's not fair for me to stand in the way of you both," she says, sincerity in her tone. "I want you both to be happy, and I wish you both the best."

God, she is so sweet.

"Thank you, Cara. That means a lot. I honestly never want to hurt you, or see you upset, so that's why Rhett and I originally said we'd just be friends. But we've been spending time together, as friends, and well—" I explain, wetting my suddenly dry lips.

"You don't have to explain yourself," she says, giving my hand a squeeze. "I appreciate you thinking of me. And I'm sorry I put you in a position where you felt like it was me or him."

"I'm pregnant," I blurt out. "That's what's changed, and Rhett knows, and you are the second person I'm telling."

"What?" she whispers, eyes widening. "You're pregnant?"

"I am. And before you ask, yes, it's Rhett's. I haven't been with anyone else in months. I know that this is a huge mess, and it's complicated, but I'm having the baby."

Cara stands up and leans over me, giving me a hug.

"Congratulations! Wait, this is good news, right?" She pulls back to look at me and I take the opportunity to study her expression, looking for any emotion that she's hiding from me. I see nothing but happiness and affection, and it warms my heart.

I exhale, relief filling me. "Yes, great news. I was so afraid to tell you, especially after we got over the first revelation. Rhett—"

"Tell me he's being supportive. If he is doing anything but being supportive, so help me God, I'll kick his ass."

I laugh, a full-belly one. And I feel the stress leave my body. Why was I so afraid of telling her? She's my sister and of course she'd be happy for me. "No, no, he is. We've actually been...dating?" I make a face because I really don't know what we've been doing.

Now it's Cara's turn to laugh. "You're pregnant with his baby, and *now* you're starting to date? A little backward, huh?"

"Are you sure you're not upset? I don't want to lose you, but this is a baby we're talking about, and I'm already in love with him or her. And I want you to be as involved as you want to be."

"I'm one hundred percent not upset." She reaches over and rubs my back.

We sit there in silence for a bit.

"Can I ask how Rhett's handling this?"

I sigh. "I just... I know it's not ideal for Rhett. We are together but not together and he's just taken over a whole MC, but I need to do what is right for me."

"And Aunty Cara will be here," she replies, sitting

back down and studying me. "I have to admit, it's a shock, though."

"You're telling me."

"And you know what? Rhett will be an amazing father, of that I have no doubt. You should see him with Sapphire, it would just make you melt. Clover was telling me how he even brought her some flowers last time he went over there because he wants to set the standard for men who will date her when she's older. I also heard that Felix went and bought her an even bigger bouquet of flowers when he found out about that, so we all know how spoiled my goddaughter is going to be."

I smile. "That is really sweet. I don't want to keep this a secret anymore. I feel so much better now it's all out in the open."

"Thank you for telling me. I'd have rather heard it from you than someone else," she says, grabbing the wine bottle. "I guess this is all mine now. I think I need it."

I laugh. "Thank you for being so wonderful, Cara. I know it's not the easiest situation for you."

"Don't worry about me. It will be fine," she assures me. "How are *you* handling everything? I mean, you're going to be a mom, wow!"

I smile big, finally allowing myself to dig into the Chinese food Cara brought over. "I'm actually good now that we've talked. I met a friend who is due around the same time, and she and I have been going to a mom group together."

"That's great! Now let's eat, and tell me how your pregnancy has been going so far. Have you been nauseous? How are you coping with work? And what's been happening with the house?"

"The house is falling apart," I grumble. "I'm going to call a real estate agent."

"Good idea."

I update her on everything that has been going on, and feel like a weight has been lifted off me.

Rhett knows.

Cara knows.

And they are both supporting me.

They might not have worked out together, but they are both individually the best people I've ever known.

Chapter Twenty-Four

Rhett

My phone buzzes with a text just as I reach the club-house.

Con: I told Cara about the baby.

Rhett: What did she say?

Neither of us wants to hurt Cara, but this is something that needed to come out.

Con: She's being supportive. We are lucky to have her. She's amazing.

I have to admit that I never once thought I would hear a current girlfriend saying that about an ex, but then again I never thought that I'd date sisters either.
But here we are.

Rhett: I'm glad. Just got to the clubhouse. I'll call you tonight.

Con: Okay.

With Cara being so accepting, I just hope that Con is willing to give me a chance and see where we can go together. I want her here, by my side, as my old lady.

Con is mine. She just doesn't know it yet.

Three days later and I'm back at Con's, waiting for her when she finishes work. I bring her flowers and food.

"Hey," she says as she hops out of her car, her long white dress blowing behind her in the wind. "You brought me flowers again?"

"Of course I did," I reply, grinning and handing them to her. "And you said you were craving a burger, so I got you that on the way, too."

"You are too good to me," she comments, kissing my cheek and then moving to unlock the door.

"I also put more money in your account, so I was thinking you could go and have a spa day or something. I don't know, treat yourself."

She stills. I know she doesn't like me giving her money, but I want her to get used to me taking care of her. She can do with it as she likes, there is no catch to it; I just want to make sure she has what she needs.

"You know you don't need to do that, Rhett. I don't expect—"

"I know you don't, Con. But I want to."

"I still haven't spent the last amount you put into my account," she admits, pushing the door open.

I reach out and hold it for her. "You can do whatever you want with it, but it's there for you."

"Thank you, Rhett. I don't want you to think that I

don't appreciate you, but really, you don't need to do any of that," she says.

We both step inside and I place the food on the counter while she puts the flowers in a vase, and then comes up to me. I wrap her in my arms and kiss the top of her head, her vanilla scent driving me crazy.

Cupping her cheek with my palm, I scan her eyes, and then lower my gaze to her lips. I want to kiss her. I don't know if she's ready for that, but when her brown eyes also drop, I take the chance and press my lips against hers.

All this time we have been acting like friends, and I've hated it, but it was better than losing her.

But all of that waiting was well worth it, and kissing her feels like home.

I lift her up in my arms and sit her back on the kitchen counter. "I want you," I whisper against her lips.

"Me too," she replies, looking into my eyes.

And then my lips are back on hers, and I carry her into her bedroom.

I need to make up for lost time tonight, and I want to take my fucking time.

She moves to straddle me and I know she can feel how hard I am underneath her.

This has been a long time coming.

I lift off her dress and it falls to the floor, exposing her bare breasts to me. They've grown since I last had her like this, and I can't stop looking. "I've missed you," I tell her.

"Me too," she replies, grinding down on my cock. "So much."

I let her ride me for a little while but then take over,

throwing her back on the bed, taking off her silky panties and spreading her thighs.

"Been wanting this for so long," I murmur, then lower my face to her pussy and start to taste her, licking her clit and driving her insane. She arches her back and lifts her thighs to my mouth, her lips falling apart as little moans escape her.

"Rhett," she whispers, and I can feel her climax building.

I hear her plea and suck on her clit, and the next moment she's moaning and calling out my name. The second I'm done, she sits up and pulls off the rest of my clothes, and then lays me back and starts to ride me again, sliding my cock into her wet pussy and moving up and down while staring into my eyes. My lips are still wet from her as she leans down and kisses me, continuing the motion with her hips. I've soon had enough of her teasing, and flip her onto her back.

We both finish together, looking into each other's eyes and wondering why the hell we ever bothered trying to stay apart.

This is where I'm meant to be.

I don't tell her I love her with words, but I kiss her sweetly afterward.

And I hope she can feel it.

"You know that I've got you covered for everything, right? I mean, you don't have to work or worry about money anymore. You can sell your house and take that money, but I know you have sentimental attachment to it, so I could pay it off for you and do it up, whatever you want. But I'd like you to move and stay with me in the clubhouse."

Probably not the best pillow talk, but it's a conversation I've been meaning to have with her.

Her eyes open. "You want me to move to the clubhouse?"

I nod. "Yeah, now that I'm president it will be harder for me to keep coming here. It would save so much time for you to be closer to me."

"I understand that," she replies. "I love my job, though, and I don't want to quit."

"I know that, but when the baby comes you won't be working," I say gently. "It's up to you, but I would love to have you at the clubhouse with me. If something happened—"

She nods. "What if we compromise and I stay here for now, and then when I'm closer to having the baby I'll move there? I have been thinking about selling my house, so I guess that works."

"Whatever works for you," I say, just happy she's agreed to come live with me in the clubhouse, even if it was temporary.

"Are you sure everyone is going to be okay with a pregnant woman living in the clubhouse? Isn't it like a giant frat house?" she asks, brow furrowing.

I laugh when I remember all the stories I heard about Aunty Faye living in the clubhouse when she was pregnant with Clover. "It is mostly men, yes. But there are some women there. Dice's woman, Leah, is there. I'll have to tell you the stories about Clover's mom when she was pregnant."

It hits me that with everything going on, I haven't

even spoken to my own parents to let them know that they are going to be grandparents. "You need to meet my mom and dad."

She winces. "Do you think they'll like me? Knowing that I'm Cara's sister? It's a bit weird, don't you think?"

"Maybe at the start, but once they get to know you I have no doubt that they will love you," I assure her. "And especially when they see how happy I am."

She rolls over onto her side, facing me. "You mean that?"

I nod. "I do."

"So just like that? We went from only being friends to me considering moving into your motorcycle club-house and meeting your parents?"

I laugh. "And just like that we're going to be parents."

"Are you only all right with this because Cara gave it the okay? I know for me that felt like a green flag," she admits. "Not that she controls our lives or anything, but I never wanted to hurt her, so when she said she wouldn't hold it against us, I felt such relief."

"I felt the same way. I don't want to hurt anyone, and I didn't want to cause a divide in the MC and among the people I love."

To be honest, though, I don't know how long I would have been able to hold out before it got too much. Let's be real, I was already "dropping in" every chance I could. I definitely think I would have gotten to a point where I would have said, "Fuck what anyone else thinks." And yeah, there would have been some reper-cussions for that.

"But I knew I wanted to be with you," I continue. "I'm glad that we have a chance to explore that now."

"Me too," she replies, snuggling into me.

I wrap my arm around her and wonder what's going to happen with Marko. All I know is that I'd do anything to protect those I love, just like the older generation of Wind Dragons had to. And along the way that might land me in prison, like it did Arrow and Irish, but that just comes with the territory.

"Even if it's going to be complicated," she whispers as if an afterthought.

I rest my hand on her stomach, cupping the tiny bump there. "It's definitely going to be interesting."

We both take a shower, and I stay for the night, the two of us getting reacquainted with each other, making love, laughing and whispering sweet nothings.

I just hope that I put her mind at ease and let her know that I'm in this with her, no matter what.

I'm not going anywhere.

Saying bye to Con the next morning is hard, but it's going to have to be this way for a while. When I'm back at the clubhouse I find myself missing her, but then remind myself that I have shit I need to be doing. The only club members living at the clubhouse full-time right now are me, Bear, Sledge, Dice and Zeke. The older men all have their own houses with their families, but will stay here now and again, or go between the two. It's a lot of fun, not going to lie, and after thinking of some of the shit we get up to, I wonder if Con is going to hate it here.

"We having a party tonight?" Bear asks, glancing down at his phone. "There's a bunch of hotties I met at Toxic who want to come over."

I shrug. "If you want to."

The men are all single except Dice—and me, even though Con and I never officially spoke about it—and they all want to have a good time and fuck around. I'm not going to get in the way of that. But with Con potentially coming to stay here when she's further along in her pregnancy, I'm looking at our daily habits in a new way.

When the party starts later that night, I take note of things that may be an issue for her.

Parties which may or may not turn into orgies. Check.

Naked women wandering around. Check.

Naked women trying to talk to me to get me to fuck them. Check.

I look over at Dice and Leah, watching them play beer pong together. At least Con will have Leah here, a nice girl who knows what goes on and still stays here. She must really love Dice.

"You want another beer?" Bear asks, sitting down next to me. "Or a shot?"

"Nah, I'm good. I think I might head to bed," I say, standing up and walking back inside. I find Zeke in the kitchen, fucking a girl against the counter, and three naked women making out in the living room.

Oh fuck, Con is going to leave my ass.

What will she think when she moves in and has to see all of this? It's normal for me, but it sure as hell won't be normal for her. Would it be a deal breaker for her?

I hope not.

I pull out my phone and send her a text message.

Rhett: I miss you. What are you doing?

Con: In bed reading. You? I miss you too.

I look over at the women, one of whom is going down on another, and decide to lie.

Rhett: Nothing much, about to go to bed. Had to deal with the cops today, so I'm beat.

Con: COPS?!? What happened?

I probably shouldn't have said anything, but I'm trying for this honesty thing. Speaking of, I should tell her about the party tonight. If I've learned anything, it's that I can't hide the truth, especially with Con. If we're going to make it, I have to always be as honest as possible.

Rhett: It sounds worse than it is. They were just questioning me about the whole thing with the Forgotten Children from a while back. I tell you about it next time I see you. Everything's fine, we're just having a party now.

Con: Party? What kind of party are you having?

Shit.

I could send her a photo, but I don't think she'd appreciate that.

Rhett: The boys are having a party.

I should have said that from the start.

Con: So you're surrounded by beautiful women all trying to get with you right now?

I think about how best to word this so I don't start a fight.

Rhett: There are women here, but I'm going to bed and leaving them to their party.

"Want to join us?" one of the women calls out, beckoning me.

I grin but shake my head and walk into my room, locking the door behind me. Yeah, I'm hard from seeing them naked, not going to lie, but Con is the only one I want and I'm not going to ruin that.

I sit in bed and do a Google search of pregnancy, what women need and what makes it easier for them.

Con: Maybe I should move into the clubhouse sooner.

I smile at her text.

Rhett: Not that you have anything to worry about… but I'd love that.

I'd be happiest if she was here with me, and I could look after her, feed her whatever she's craving and know that she's safe. I know she loves her job, but things have changed. And she doesn't need to work anymore.

I put my headphones on to block out the music and the loud moans from the party and go to bed.

And when I fall asleep, I dream of Con.

Chapter Twenty-Five

Con

"What kind of stuff goes on in the clubhouse?" I ask Cara when she comes over the next morning. I'd spent the morning chatting to Olivia on the phone, and only ended the call when Cara got here. We are planning on catching up soon and going out to lunch together.

Cara chokes on her hash brown. "Ummm."

"And don't censor for me at all," I tell her.

She clears her throat. "I mean, there's usually women there. Women who would do anything to be with the bikers, hoping to be an old lady. They like to hang around. And they have some wild parties where anything goes. You can't be a prude if you're going to go to them."

"I see. Do you think I could live at the clubhouse?" I ask, gauging her reaction. "Rhett wants me to."

Cara shrugs. "I think you could live there, if you don't mind orgies."

Now it's my time to choke. "Do you think Rhett would cheat on me at these parties? I mean we're not officially together, but we sorta are."

She gives me a look. "You're totally together and I don't think so," Cara says. "I mean, I thought he cheated on me, but turns out he didn't. So…"

"I don't know. How am I supposed to relax knowing that he's at the clubhouse with beautiful women, some he must have already slept with?"

"You trust him," she suggests.

"There was a party at the clubhouse last night," I explain, taking a sip of my orange juice and leaning back in my seat. "And it's obviously something they do a lot, and I don't know how I should react."

"You have to trust him, and your relationship," she says, looking down at my stomach. "And you are pregnant with his child. He'd be a total asshole if he did."

"Apparently men cheat on their pregnant partners the most," I say in a dry tone. "I've read that somewhere before. It's a thing."

"I think you should just speak to him and tell him how you're feeling," she suggests, tone gentle. "Definitely talk to him. And I think you should go to the clubhouse and experience it for yourself. Meet the members. See if you can live with all of it."

I nod. "You're right, I should just go there. Maybe I'll surprise him. Will you come with me? Random surprise road trip to see if my…can I even call him my man?"

"Safe to say he's your man," Cara adds. "And yeah, why not? I can come."

"Really?"

"Sure. Fuck it. I'll tell Decker I won't be home until evening. I'll call Clover and see if she wants to come, too."

I grin.

Clover tells us she'll meet us there. We pack up Cara's car and then head to the Dragon's Lair.

"Are we allowed to just walk in?" I ask Cara when we get there.

She laughs. "Hell yeah we are. This is our second home."

We get out of the car and there are two men standing out the front next to their motorcycles. "Hey, Zeke," Cara calls out. "Bear."

"Cara, what a nice surprise," Zeke purrs, checking her out.

"Keep looking at me like that if you want to die," Cara replies, still smiling.

Bear slaps Zeke on the chest. "Be respectful unless you want to deal with Rake."

"Not just Rake—you'll have every member coming down on your ass," she says, standing in front of him. "Where's Prez?"

"He's inside," Bear replies, looking over me curiously. "He know you're here?"

"It's a surprise," I say, smiling and flashing him my teeth.

"She's his woman, she doesn't need an invitation," Cara says, arching her brow. She takes my hand and leads me inside. "Well, looks like the party is still going." We pass the living room and see naked bodies fast asleep there.

I start to feel a little sick at the sight. Why are they out here in public? Can't they go to their rooms? Is this going to be my view every time I have breakfast?

I don't even know what to say right now.

Rhett comes out of his room, bare chested and in nothing but a pair of basketball shorts. His eyes widen when he sees me, and he smiles. "Con? What are you doing here?"

"Surprise," I say, glancing around as beautiful women in bikinis step into the house through the sliding door. At least they have something on. All while Rhett is wearing no shirt, showing off his six-pack abs and delicious body for all the thirsty women to see.

I don't love it.

"Welcome to the clubhouse."

"Can we talk?" I ask him.

"Yeah. Come on, we can talk in my room."

I look at Cara, who nods, so I follow behind him down a long hallway. He opens one of the doors on the right, and I step inside to a modern, tidy bedroom, even bigger than my own, one with a massive king-size bed, and a TV that almost covers the whole wall.

Not what I was expecting.

This room could be in a display home, aside from the few items of clothing on the floor in the corner.

"I just wanted to come here today and just see for myself what it's like here, and if I could live here. I asked Cara some questions, and I didn't love the answers."

"I'll bet," he replies under his breath.

"I mean, how would you feel if I was hanging out with men I've slept with before every other night? Men who are good-looking and barely clothed?" I ask him.

A muscle ticks in his jaw. "Yeah, I'd probably end up in prison."

"Exactly. So I'm sure you can see this isn't an ideal

situation for me. There are so many beautiful women around here."

"The most beautiful one is mine," he says, taking my hand in his. "I'm not going to mess with us, Con. You have nothing to worry about."

"Okay, but what would you do if we had just had a big fight, or were going through a rough patch or we hadn't had sex in a while? Would you be tempted?" I ask quietly. "It's easy to say no when we're happy and still in the honeymoon stage. But I need to know that you will say no even if we're not."

Relationships go through ups and downs, and I don't ever want to feel like if we have a fight or something he's going to turn to other women. I need to be able to trust him and vice versa for this to work. We're bringing a child into the mix, and everything is up against us. We need to stay strong, communicate and be honest with each other or we're just going to end up breaking up and our child will have a broken family. I also don't know if this is the best environment to have a baby in, especially if there are rowdy parties going on, but I'll deal with everything as it comes.

"I promise that I will always choose you, and that I will be honest with you at all times, okay? I want this to work, too. I'm not perfect, but I'm trying," he says, lifting my fingers to his lips and kissing them. "I don't want anything except you. Now, come on, let me give you a proper tour of the clubhouse since the last time you were here it didn't go so well."

He shows me around the place, introduces me to everyone properly, as his woman, and then we order in some food and sit around their newly installed pool and enjoy the sunshine. The men are all nice, and a few of them make conversation with me.

Cara's parents show up, and I meet them all for the first time. I know this whole thing has to be awkward for them, especially Rake and Bailey, so I make sure to not make any public displays of affection with Rhett.

"It's nice to see you and Cara are getting close," Bailey says, watching me. "I have to admit when she told me about you, I wasn't so sure if it was a good idea or not."

"I understand. Wade was not a great guy," I reply, watching Cara sitting next to her dad, the two of them laughing about something. "And I know how weird it must be that Rhett and I…"

Bailey laughs. "Yes, it was. It is. But Cara is happy with Decker, and like she says, she wants the two of you to be happy, too. You're nothing like Wade," she says quietly, relief in her tone. "I'm sorry, I know he's your dad and I shouldn't speak ill of the dead—"

"It's okay, I know who he was," I reply, smiling sadly. "He wasn't always a good person, so I make sure that I at least try to be. And I'd never intentionally do anything to hurt Cara. She's wonderful."

"She is," Bailey agrees, smiling at her daughter.

Rhett's parents, Tia and Talon, show up and I get to finally meet both of them.

"Mom, Dad, this is Con. Con, these are my parents," Rhett introduces.

"It's lovely to meet you," I say to them, smiling. I feel a little nervous of course. Everyone knows each and every drama I've been through since meeting Rhett, and I'm pregnant without even having properly met most of his family.

"You too," Tia replies, taking my hand in hers. "And congratulations on your pregnancy. I have to admit it was a bit of a shock when Rhett told me."

"Understatement," Talon says, shaking his head.

Tia taps him on his arm. "But a blessing. We are both so excited to be grandparents."

I smile. "Thank you, I know the whole thing has been a surprise, so I appreciate you all being so kind about it."

"We just want everyone to be happy," she replies, glancing over at everyone in the pool. "And I had no idea we were having a spontaneous pool party today."

"No one did," Bailey laughs. "But it's so nice to see all of them."

"Isn't it?" Tia whispers, hugging Rhett and smiling up at her son. I can see how much she loves and adores him, and it's beautiful to see.

Tia and I sit down and get to know each other a little better, and I think my child has lucked out with his or her grandparents, because they are wonderful people. Which is good, because they'll have no one on my side.

And you know what?

I guess the clubhouse isn't so bad after all.

My child will get to grow up around family, good, loyal people, and will be so loved.

The village all mothers need to help raise their child? I've got it, right here.

"So what do you think?" Cara asks, she and Clover sitting next to me looking out at the pool. Clover arrived a few minutes ago.

"You know I don't talk much about my childhood, but Wade used to bring women home all the time when my mom was working. Different women. And he didn't really hide…what he was doing. They would do drugs, whatever they wanted. No one cared that I was there. The men here aren't like that. The second it turned to a family environment, everyone stopped and the naked women all left. I appreciate that. And to think my child is going to be loved by so many people…it feels good."

Clover studies me. "I'm sorry you were stuck with Wade as your father. Cara was lucky to get away from him."

I nod silently. "I'm glad you did, Cara."

She reaches over and takes my hand. "And I'm glad you found your way back to me."

I am too.

Chapter Twenty-Six

Rhett

Seeing everyone I care about all together and happy under my roof makes me feel pretty damn good. Especially observing my mom and Con chatting. It's so important to me that the two of them get along and like each other, so watching them getting to know each other and laugh together is really something. These are moments I won't forget.

I see Natty arrive and greet everyone. She says something to Con, and the two of them have a little chat before she comes over to us.

"I'm sorry, but what did I just see? Was that the famously stubborn Natalie Ward saying…sorry?" Cara teases.

Natty hugs her and kisses her cheek. "Well, everyone has made up now, so I might as well get on board. Plus, I was really mean. I must have been hangry that night."

I pull her under my arm and mess up her hair. "Nice to see you make an appearance."

"Nice to see you too, Prez," she replies, sounding impressed. "My my, haven't we come up in the world."

I laugh. "I have, and I'm looking forward to you being our lawyer when we get into shit."

She grins. "I'm ready and waiting. Let's place bets on who is going to be the first person who needs me."

Cara points to me. "This guy. He's out here in the middle of all the drama. You name it, it's happened. This month alone."

"Yeah, and I still have someone following me," I mutter low enough so no one hears me. I saw the same car following me again yesterday, but I still haven't figured out who this woman is. If I'm being honest, with everything going on I'd almost forgotten about it.

Natty smirks. "So I've heard. Looks like it's time for our generation to take over. Faye told me I can handle all the club business now and only call her in if it's important."

"Maybe you'll find your own biker to call yours," Clover says suggestively.

Natty makes a face. "Clo, you know they aren't my type. When I think of a biker, I think of Dad or your dad or Rhett." She visibly shakes off her disgust. So dramatic. "I'm going to end up with a lawyer, or a banker. Someone who wears suits every day and looks damn good in them."

"Well," Cara starts, "none of us actually ended up with a biker."

"I did," Con says as she comes back over, and it's the first time she says it with confidence. I think I fall in love with her in that moment.

"Damn right you did." I lean over to kiss her.

"Awww…" everyone coos, and I give them all the finger while I show everyone that Con is mine.

"Either way, guess you're going to be busy then, Natty," Cara replies, then picks up her sister and throws her into the pool, laughing.

Natty resurfaces and spits water out of her mouth. "I'm going to kill you!"

Faye arrives, smiling happily as she sees us all together. Clover runs to hug her mother, who is saddened when she hears Fire is at home with Felix.

"I didn't know it was going to turn into a family pool party," Clover says. "For all we knew, Con was going to run out of here screaming."

Con laughs. "There's still time."

I can't remember the last time I have felt this relaxed. I know my mom was a little shocked and confused by the whole Con situation and with her being pregnant, but I hope now that they have met and spoken to each other that this can just become our new normal.

My mom will always love Cara, and hell, so will I, but she can also grow to love Con like her own daughter, too. Through this child, we will always be tied, the whole lot of us, and we need to make the best of the situation.

I sit down with my mom, Faye, Bailey and Con. "Pregnant and moving into the clubhouse," Faye comments, smiling to herself. "Doesn't that sound familiar? Do you know what you're getting into, Con?"

"Don't scare her off," I grumble.

"She's moving here willingly," Cara's mom points out, laughing. "Rhett didn't have to track her down in a hotel and bring her back."

"I feel like that makes it worse, somehow," Con adds, making the women laugh harder.

"I used to break into the men's rooms and clean them when I was nesting. It drove them crazy. I had no boundaries," Faye says, tone amused.

"Had?" Mom asks, smirking.

Faye laughs. "But you know what? The men were there for me, and they loved Clover so much. They still do. And everyone will love your baby just as much."

Con smiles, happiness in her brown eyes. "I think that sounds pretty wonderful."

"You need to be strong, though, Con. Hold your ground. Trust your gut. This life isn't for the faint of heart. You have to learn how to read people," Mom says.

"What do you mean?" Con asks, genuinely taking in all that these three powerhouses have to offer.

"You have to be careful on who you trust and let into your life. You're now the old lady of the president of the Wind Dragons MC. The Wind Dragons and probably the Knights of Fury down south are the biggest MCs in Southern California. People will want to get to Rhett, and they'll try through you."

Con nods. "I'll be on the lookout. I'm a fighter, that's one thing about me."

"Good," Faye replies. "And you already have Cara and Clover on your side, which would have been the hardest battle for anyone else."

"Still working on Clover," Con admits.

They all laugh. "She's coming around," Faye says, and rubs Con's arm.

"She has me on her side," I remind them all. "So she has nothing to worry about."

The women all share a look, smiling at each other.

Tracker's fifteen-year-old daughter, Annalise, runs

over to me. The girl is a female version of her dad, but is sweet like her mom, Lana. "Hi, Uncle Rhett. The pizza man is here. Dad told me not to answer the door here, so someone else has to get it."

Bear overhears and gets up. "I'm on it."

We all eat and spend the rest of the day by the pool, and it's really nice. Everyone is welcoming to Con, and I feel proud having her here, and making her a part of our extended family.

All is going well until I step into the kitchen and overhear a conversation my mom is having with Con. "You're brave moving in here; I don't think I could have."

"Mom—" I quickly interject, trying to cut her off then and there.

"I'm just being honest," she replies, rolling her eyes. "If there's anything I can help with, Cara, let me know." Her eyes widen as she realizes the slip. "Con. I mean Con, not Cara. Sorry, force of habit."

We all go silent, tension filling the room.

Shit.

I clear my throat. And to think, everything was going so well. "Thanks, Mom."

She keeps talking, making it worse. "Well, you can't blame me. Cara was the only real girlfriend you ever had and they kind of look a little similar—"

Con looks like she wants to run.

"I don't think they do," Faye says. "They have similar features, but they're each beautiful in their own way." I give Aunt Faye a thank-you look.

"Con, you must take after your mother, who, if I remember, was a beauty," Bailey says, trying to cover for my mother.

Con forces a smile. "Um, speaking of Cara, I'm going to go see what she's doing."

The second she leaves, I groan. "Mom, seriously?"

"I'm sorry, it just slipped out!" she replies, wincing. "Even their names both start with *C*."

"T, you made it so much worse," Bailey says as she shakes her head.

"I didn't mean it! I froze and then I didn't know what to say, so then I just kept talking and made it worse. I'm sorry, Rhett. I asked her if she would like to go to dinner, and she said yes."

I scrub my hand down my face. "Yeah, before you called her my ex-girlfriend's name."

She sighs. "I will apologize."

"Please do. Where's Dad?" I ask her.

"He's out the front still talking to Zeke. It's so weird coming here and seeing all these new faces."

"The old ones are still around."

"I know," she says, stepping to me and touching my cheek. "And how are you doing, my son?"

"I'm good, better now that Con is here. I want her to move in here, so please stop scaring her away."

"Overprotective, just like your father," Mom says in an amused tone. "I'm going to go and find him before I say something else stupid."

I find Con outside talking with my dad. I watch them for a few seconds, appreciating the moment. He must say something funny, most likely at my expense, and she throws her head back and laughs, making me smile.

This is all new for her, and I just need to let her know how wanted she is.

And that just like the club—she's now mine.

"So what do you think? When are you moving in here?" I ask Con once everyone starts to leave and the sun starts to set.

"It was a pretty beautiful day, minus all the naked women," she says, rolling her eyes. "Your parents are so nice; I'm so happy I finally got to meet them. And no one yelled at me or called me the Wish version of Cara, so that's always nice."

I kiss her cheek. "No one will ever disrespect you again, Con. No one. You have my word on that."

"The word of the president," she teases, kissing my cheek. "I better get ready to go. When will I see you next?"

"Do you have to go?" I ask. "Why don't you stay here a night or two, and I'll take you back home?"

"I don't know. I came with Cara—I made her come here and I don't want to ditch her now," she replies, brow furrowing.

"They won't care," I assure her, then call out, "Cara! Clo! Can I keep Con here? Do you care if she stays?"

Cara laughs. "You can stay here, Con. You wanted to see what the clubhouse is like, so you might as well stay and get the full experience."

"If you don't mind," Con says, going and hugging them. "Thank you both for coming with me. You guys are the best."

"Anytime," Clover says.

"It was nice to have everyone together. You both

enjoy yourself. I'd say be safe but, well." Cara points to Con's belly.

"Nice, Cara," I deadpan. "Thank you for bringing her here. And thank you for being…you."

"No worries," she replies with a grin. "I like seeing you both so happy."

She gets in her car and I take my woman back inside, and back into my room. I'm so proud of how she has handled everything, of us for communicating, and her just getting along with the whole MC.

I slowly undress her, teasing her with gentle kisses down her skin. I can't get enough of her, and I want to show her how fucking happy I am to have her here with me right now.

I show her with my mouth, dipping my finger inside her pussy while I eat her out. One, then two fingers.

She comes.

Twice.

And then with my cock.

I lightly wrap my fingers around her neck, waiting for her permission, and she nods, putting her hand encouragingly over mine. I squeeze gently, and she gets even wetter, so I know how much she likes that. I squeeze harder. I come in her from behind, with her gripping the sheets, my name on her lips.

Yeah, I'm not going to ruin this for anything.

Chapter Twenty-Seven

Con

I wake up to breakfast in bed. "Is this a special treatment to get me to stay here or is this going to be an every morning thing?" I tease.

"Every morning there's not a club emergency," he replies, smirking. "This was my first time making poached eggs, so I hope they were okay."

"Thank you, they look perfect," I say, sitting up and fixing the pillow behind my back. "So what do you have on today? What does a Monday in the life of the MC president look like?"

"Well, unless something needs my attention I will be spending the day with you," he replies, kissing the top of my head.

"You never told me what happened with the cops," I say, realizing that I forgot to ask last night when everyone left.

"They are looking for Marko, asked if I had seen him. I said no," he explains, sitting down on the edge of the bed as I eat. "They had heard that the MC and the FC had some kind of altercation, so I'm guessing members of the FC who are still loyal to Marko are talking to the cops, looking for him."

"And do you know anything?"

He shakes his head. "No one knows where he is." After a brief silence, he continues. "You know there may come a time where I will commit a crime, to protect someone I love. Are you going to be able to live with that?"

"Well, this got deep quickly," I joke, trying to lighten the mood. "I don't know, Rhett. I want to be able to support you, but I don't know if I want to hear all the details about things. Let me think about this. I'm only new to this world, so I'd like to go slow when it comes to the information you share, please. I appreciate your willingness to be honest with me, though. Know I will always have your back and be loyal to you. That I am sure of."

"Good," he whispers. "Mom invited us over for lunch, and then I thought maybe we could go for a ride to the beach or something. What do you think?"

"Sounds perfect."

He smiles and jumps in the shower while I finish eating my bacon, eggs, avocado and toast, hoping that I can be what he needs.

It's a big responsibility being with Rhett, and it means that I too need to dedicate my life to the MC and the people in it. But yesterday being with everyone around the pool showed me that these are people worth protecting.

This is his family, and now it's also becoming mine. I just need to be strong, strong as all the women he's been surrounded with his whole life.

And strong for my child.

But like my mom said, I also need to trust my gut, and while I love the clubhouse and the MC, I don't know if I want to live there and give up the life I have been building. It's just a big adjustment.

After breakfast, I shower and get ready for the day, then head outside by the pool to enjoy a little sunshine. I sit down on one of the sun chairs only to realize I'm not alone.

In fact, there are two people in the pool. Naked.

"Oh my God, I'm so sorry!" I call out, running back inside. I can hear them laughing behind me. They were having sex and I literally walked out there and sat down, like I was about to enjoy the show. I'm *mortified.*

Sitting at the kitchen table, I ponder my new life and how I got here.

"What's wrong?" Rhett asks as he sits next to me.

"Nothing," I say a little too quickly.

"Con, your face is bright red. Tell me."

I clear my throat. "I went outside to enjoy the sunshine."

"Okay?"

"And then I sat down on the sun chairs—"

"Okay," he repeats, brow furrowing in confusion.

"And I was just looking around until I realized Bear was in there with a woman. Naked. In the middle of fucking each other. And I sat down there."

Rhett goes still and then bursts out laughing. "They probably got more turned on knowing they had an audience."

"Rhett," I growl. "I'm not a prude by any means, but how am I supposed to see all this and then look the men in the eye? Like there are clearly no boundaries here. Can I walk around naked, too?"

The humor leaves his face. "No, I'm the only one who gets to see all that. I mean, feel free to wear what you want, but you are not walking around here butt naked. I share everything with my men, except you. You are mine and mine only."

"Then that goes both ways," I state, lifting my chin. "Fair?"

"That's fine with me."

"What about a thong bikini?" I ask, feeling amused.

He shrugs. "Whatever you want to wear is fine with me. Your body. And I know how to fight."

I laugh at that.

"And yes, the men aren't shy and will do what they want to do, but that's the freedom they get here. No judgment. As long as they aren't hurting anyone," he continues.

"What about when the baby comes? Do you want him or her exposed to that at a young age?"

Rhett stiffens. "When the baby comes, we'll both move somewhere close by and I'll just keep a room here."

I can't get over how much thought he's put into this. It makes me feel like everything is going to be okay, if and when I do decide to move into the clubhouse. It's just so different here, and I know that eventually I would get used to it. But I'm going to have to anticipate some awkward moments before I feel a little more comfortable with the idea.

"Well," I say with a sigh. "I guess me and the Wind

Dragons members are going to get very well acquainted then."

Rhett grins and leans closer to kiss me. "Not *that* well acquainted."

Bear sticks his head into the room, towel wrapped around his waist. "Get a room, you two."

I lift my head. "You're kidding, right? You can have sex out there, but we can't kiss?"

Bear laughs, and his towel almost falls off. "You can do whatever you like. Don't worry, I like to watch, too."

My jaw drops open. He winks at me and goes on his merry way.

I turn to find Rhett watching me with amusement in his eyes. "You don't have to do anything you are uncomfortable with, you know that, right? You have nothing to worry about. I don't care what they are doing—all I care about is you." He kisses my cheek. "Pleasing you." He moves to kiss the side of my neck. "Your little moans in my ear. I get so hard just thinking about them. Mmm. Maybe we should go back to my room. Or maybe you should let me take you here, right now."

"Here?" I ask, eyes fluttering back open.

He laughs, carries me in his arms and takes me back to his room, locking the door behind him.

Chapter Twenty-Eight

Rhett

We have lunch with my mom, and then I take Con for a ride to the beach. I love having her here. And I hope fucking Bear didn't make her change her mind with his pool escapades this morning. I wanted to ease her into all the shit that goes on in the clubhouse; instead she's seen mostly nudity and sex since she got here. At least the family all showed up so she saw that side of it, too.

It's not all sex and orgies here—we also have family cookouts, do charity runs and fundraisers and spend a lot of quality time together. It's not all bad, and I hope she can see that. I mean, she's still here, so I guess that's a good sign.

I spoke to Bear about toning it down, and he wasn't happy. I get it, it's been this way for the past few years when all the OGs' kids grew up. Bear doesn't realize that for a good chunk of my childhood it was a clean house, a family house. But as president, now I can make calls they might not like, and they will have to fall into line. I just hope it all falls into place for me.

* * *

It takes me a few days before I admit that I'm struggling with Con being so far away. She's back at her job now, and I know she loves working there, but I want her in my bed every night and I fucking miss her.

Rhett: I think you need to quit and move in now. What do you think?

Con: And what will I do in the clubhouse all day? Wait in your bedroom for you?

Rhett: That sounds nice. Maybe put something sexy on.

Con: ...

Rhett: I'm kidding. But isn't growing a child in your belly enough of a job? You can just relax and enjoy your pregnancy.

What woman actually wants to work when she's all pregnant and tired? If she moves in now, I can spoil her, look after her and get her anything that she needs.

Con: You know I have to work to pay for shit, right? My mortgage, for one, and everything else that comes with being alive.

Rhett: I told you I will take care of it all. You don't have to worry about money anymore.

Con: I don't feel comfortable with that. I can't ask for you to pay for everything for me. It wouldn't feel right.

Rhett: You are my woman and about to have my child. It's my job to support you. And it's not like I don't have the money to do so. There will be plenty for you to do here as my old lady. You can sort out all the charity fundraising events.

She doesn't reply for about twenty minutes, so I know she must be thinking about it, but I figure she'd enjoy doing the charity work. The previous old ladies did, and it gives her something to do for the MC.

Con: I don't want to leave my job just yet. I'm pregnant, but I can still work for a few more months at least. I do want to sell my house, though. It's falling apart.

My stomach drops.
I understand that the clubhouse isn't the best place for a pregnant woman, but *I'm* here. Faye did it. Why can't Con?
Did their talk with her put her off?

Con: I'm sorry, Rhett. I still want to be with you. I'm just not ready to move just yet.

Rhett: I'm disappointed, but I understand.

Con: Do you?

Rhett: It's not what I want, but if it makes you happier

to stay there, then we will make it work. Sell your house. I'll buy us a new one near Cara.

Con: I'll put in the money from the house sale.

Rhett: No, you can put that into savings for you.

Con: Stubborn ass.

Rhett: Let me get my way with something at least.

Con: I trust you. We can make this work.

Rhett: We can.

I want to be there for her in some way. And don't get me wrong, I'll still visit her as much as I can, but I'm pretty unhappy I won't be seeing her every day. At least if she lives near Cara and Decker, they can be close by in case of emergency.

Fuck.

This isn't going the way I had planned.

But we've come such a long way in such a short time, and I just know in my gut that she is who I'm meant to be with.

Someone has to sacrifice, and I guess right now it's going to be me.

"Why do you look like someone kicked your puppy?" Dice asks, taking the seat next to me.

"Con doesn't want to move in."

"Ahh. Well, it might be for the better, because I just saw that car circling around here again. I don't know who that woman is or what she wants, but we need to find out."

I nod. I've been so distracted with everything going on, I'd forgotten. Or maybe because it's just one woman, I don't know. "Did someone sleep with her and then piss her off or something?"

Dice laughs. "I don't know, maybe we should ask the Casanovas in there."

Dice is right.

There is shit going on here, so maybe it's best if Con is away from it all.

For now, anyway.

Chapter Twenty-Nine

Con

"Hey," Cara says with a warm smile. "I've got Clover, Fire and a giant basket of food in the car. Surprise! We are kidnapping you to go on a picnic."

I smile widely. "That sounds amazing. Let me text my friend Olivia to see if she can meet us. Do you mind? She and I were supposed to meet up."

"Sure, the more the merrier."

I send a text to Olivia, excited she'll finally get to meet everyone, and pile into Clover's car, sitting in the back next to Fire.

"Hi, Con!" she says happily.

"Hello, Fire. Don't you look cute today?" I reply, admiring her beige dress and little black leather boots.

"I do," she responds, making me laugh.

"She has her mother's ego," Cara teases from the front.

"A little bit of confidence isn't a bad thing," Clover responds with amusement in her tone.

"How are you, Clover?" I ask.

She turns back to look at me. "Not so bad, and yourself?" Clover has slowly started warming up to me, but I can tell she still has her guard up. Clover is loyal to a fault, and it's not a bad trait to have. I just hope one day she will trust me, too.

We arrive at a beautiful park I've never been to before, with big trees, and a playground for Fire.

I help unclip Fire from her car seat, and Clover picks her up while Cara grabs the picnic basket and blanket. I can tell by their little setup that this is something they must do a lot, and it's a pretty cute idea. I help Cara put down the picnic blanket and set up the food, including a little platter on a wooden serving board.

"You are well prepared," I say, feeling bad that I didn't bring anything.

"Yep. Cheese, crackers and good company is my happy place, and I'm not going to let anyone ruin that," she replies with a grin. "I'm glad you're here with us."

"Me too."

We all sit down and Fire takes my hand, wanting me to take her to the playground. I check with Clover if it's okay first, and when she agrees I put Fire on the swing and push her gently back and forth. Clover and Cara join us, and we all play with Fire for a little while before settling in on the grass for a snack.

My phone buzzes with a text.

Rhett: Where are you? I'm at your house.

Con: I'm at the park with Clover, Cara and Fire.

Rhett: I'm coming.

I place my phone down on the tartan blanket. "Rhett just asked where we were, and said he was coming here. Does he know where this place is?"

Cara nods. "Yeah, we come here often."

"I'm still getting used to you two being openly together. It's still a little weird," Clover admits.

"Clo," Cara inserts, giving Clover a look that says to let it go. "This is a picnic for Con, and this is our new norm. We need to get used to it."

"You are a saint," I hear Clover mutter under her breath.

She really is.

Fire clears the tension in the air by coming and sitting next to me to eat her slice of cheese. And it's not long before we can hear the rumble of Rhett's motorcycle. We all watch as he gets off it, takes off his helmet, flicking back his long blond hair like he's in a damn commercial, and heads our way.

Clover is right, though. I'm definitely feeling a little awkward. Yeah, we were all at the clubhouse, but everyone was there. This is a lot more intimate, without as many distractions.

I see Olivia get out of her car and wave. She's been a bit depressed these past few days, and we haven't been able to connect. I'm glad she's able to join us. I think she'd fit in really well. Hopefully meeting the girls will cheer her up a little, because they are both hilarious, with big personalities.

"Who is that?" Clover asks straightaway, concern in her tone.

"That's Olivia. She's the new friend of mine I was telling Cara about," I explain, getting up and walking toward her. Fire joins me, holding my hand. I look down at her and smile.

When I look back up Olivia has stopped about five feet away from me, a weird expression on her face. She looks sad, but also angry.

"Is everything okay?" I call out to her, brow furrowing. Maybe now wasn't the right time to encourage her to be social. Maybe I should have spent time with her alone so she can tell me what's going on in her life that's making her so distant.

She suddenly pulls her hands out from behind her back, revealing a gun and aiming it right at me.

"Olivia?" Fear and confusion fill me. What the hell is happening right now? I can hear Cara and Clover behind me and Rhett yell my name.

"Fire, honey, come back to Mommy," I hear Clover say as I push her behind my leg as much as possible without moving. Dread fills my stomach. Something is very, very wrong. And someone is going to get hurt, but it's not going to be Fire. She holds on to my leg as if she can also sense the danger of the situation and freezes in place.

"She's not going anywhere," Olivia screeches. "Sorry, Con. I didn't want to have to do this. But my son died. Did you know that? My firstborn died. And now my baby…is gone, too." Tears drip from her eyes.

She lost both of her kids? I'm so sorry for her; I wouldn't wish that on my worst enemy. But I'm still confused.

What does that have to do with me? With why she is pointing a gun at me?

I don't understand. I thought that we were friends.

I trusted her.

"I lost my babies, and now you need to feel the same pain." I think she's mentally been pushed over the edge, and under any other circumstances I'd understand and grieve with her. But I refuse to let her anguish kill me or anyone I care about.

In a split second, everything happens at once. Fire moves out from behind my legs, Rhett grabs Olivia from behind and the gun goes off. Instinctually, I turn my back and throw myself on top of Fire.

The bullet hits me in the back of my shoulder, and I feel an agonizing pain shoot through my body. I look down at Fire, checking her body to make sure that she's unharmed.

Thank goodness she's okay. The bullet only hit me.

Cara rushes over to me and tells me to hold still as she puts pressure on the wound. Fire is crying and is picked up in her mother's arms, while Clover stares stoically at Rhett and Olivia. Rhett manages to pin Olivia down and disarm her.

"Cara, call an ambulance!" I hear him yell. Fire holds my free hand and Clover and Cara work to try to stop the bleeding. I remember them talking to me, but it all becomes so hazy.

"Stay with me, Con," Clover says, and it's the last thing I hear before it all goes black.

I wake up in a hospital bed, Rhett, Cara and Clover in my room, sitting in silence. When Rhett realizes that I'm awake, he quickly moves to me and takes my hand in his.

"Hey, how are you feeling?" he asks, smiling at seeing me awake.

"Like a train hit me. What happened?" I ask, gathering my thoughts.

"You got shot and then passed out. You lost a fair bit of blood, but the doctor said you will be all right."

"The baby?" My hand instantly goes to my stomach.

"He's fine," Rhett says with pride.

"He?" I smile.

"The doctor told me it was a boy. I hope it's okay."

I squeeze his hand. A son. "It's more than okay."

Cara takes my other hand. "I'm so sorry this happened, Con. You said this woman was your friend? Why did she shoot you? They've arrested her, but she won't talk to the cops."

"I don't know," I whisper. "The whole thing is insane. I met her at the doctor's office—she was pregnant too and we've been in contact ever since. We joined a mom group and everything. She said she lost the baby, but why did she shoot me over that?"

"We are trying to work that out. She is obviously grieving and not mentally in a good place right now," Cara comments, then gives my hand a squeeze and says, "We'll give you two some privacy and come back to visit you later. Let me know if you want me to bring you anything."

"I will, thank you."

Before she leaves, Clover takes my hand and looks into my eyes. "Thank you so much for protecting Fire. She would have been shot if it wasn't for you. I owe you everything, Con."

"No, you don't, Clo."

"I do. And I've been so horrible to you… I'm sorry, Con. I can't thank you enough for protecting my daughter."

"I hope you can try to trust me a little now."

"You're going to be a wonderful mother and I'm going to be here for you every step of the way." She wipes the tears away from her eyes.

They both leave Rhett and I alone.

I notice all the flowers in my room. I rarely get flowers, and now there are four bouquets around me.

"I brought you the roses, Cara and Decker the sunflowers. Atlas brought you in the wildflower bunch from the Knights of Fury MC, and the orchids are from everyone at your work," Rhett explains, eyes twinkling. "And Clover and Felix brought you doughnuts, just to be different."

"Clover does like giving out doughnuts," I reply.

Rhett smiles, but then sighs. "I'm so sorry for what happened today, Con. We are still trying to fill in the missing pieces. You said Olivia was your friend, and I knew I had seen her from somewhere. She has been following me."

"Olivia?" I clarify, confused. "Why would she do that?" Then again, why would she shoot me? There's obviously something going on here that I'm missing.

"It's all my fault. I should have stayed away from you completely, then you'd be safe. You could have moved on with your life—"

"My life was nothing before all of you walked into it," I cut him off. "I had a shit job, no family, not many friends. These flowers around me? They are the most I've received in my entire life."

I wouldn't want him to walk away.

And not just him. Cara, everyone. I love having them all in my life no matter how complicated it gets.

I've been targeted twice now, and I wouldn't change a thing. If that's the price I pay for family and for loyalty, I'll take it. And if any one of them is in danger, I'll be with everyone else, helping them, too.

"You were shot," he says in a dry tone, shaking his head. "Can you imagine how I feel? I don't want anything like that to happen to you again. I was terrified."

"So was I," I admit. "But I'd take that bullet any day to protect the rest of you. And when Olivia shot me, I don't know if you heard, but she said that she lost both her children so now it was only fair that I lost mine. Does that mean anything to you?"

"So she wasn't targeting you, exactly—she wanted our child to die," he says, face going pale. "I could have lost both of you. Before I even got the chance to…"

He trails off and goes silent.

"You didn't lose us. We are both right here."

A doctor steps into the room, clipboard in her hand. "How are you feeling?"

"Okay."

"I'm going to do a check on your vitals."

"I'll wait outside," Rhett says, and I know he's upset about the new revelation.

"Is the baby okay?" I ask her.

She nods. "Yes, the baby is fine. You're lucky you only got shot in the arm."

I look at my bandaged arm. "I know." If the bullet had hit me anywhere else… I don't even want to think about what would've happened.

Cara comes back a little later and sits down next to me. "How are you holding up?"

"Not too bad," I say. "I mean, it could have been a lot worse. It was my first time being shot, and it's safe to say I hope that never happens again."

She smiles, and reaches out and takes my hand. "You saved Fire, Con."

I nod, swallowing hard. "I did what anyone would have." Olivia wasn't a good shot, and if I hadn't moved that bullet would have hit Fire and not me. "I'd do the same for anyone I love," I whisper, wrapping my arms around myself. "I'd have done the same for you."

I feel so vulnerable in this moment, so seen.

"And I for you," she replies, eyes gentle.

She sits with me for the next hour and we just chat. Rhett comes back in. And then Clover comes in with Fire, and they all sit with me so that I'm not alone.

Olivia almost made me lose all of this.

And I need to make sure she won't try to do it again.

Chapter Thirty

Rhett

Con settles in at Cara's while she recovers, and I start looking for houses for sale nearby.

"Hey," Cara says as she opens the door. Her eyes widen as they land on the new patch on my cut. "I forgot to say congratulations, President. I know it's everything that you ever wanted."

"Thank you," I say. I don't know why but the words *be careful what you wish for* play in my head.

She opens her door wider. "Come on in, Con is in the living room."

I smile at her. "Thanks."

I find Con eating a bowl of ice cream, covered in a blanket and watching *The Little Mermaid* on the TV.

Cara always knew how to make someone feel safe.

"Hey," I murmur, sitting down at her feet. "How are you feeling?"

"I'm okay."

Sitting on the couch together, I move to lift her feet onto my lap, but then I remember where we are. Cara is obviously accepting the situation, but that doesn't mean that I want to make her feel uncomfortable. Slow steps. "I love this movie."

Con's lip twitches. "You telling me the president of the Wind Dragons MC loves Disney movies?"

"That's exactly what I'm telling you."

Cara comes out of hiding and sits in the single leather chair. "So, I'm aware this is going to be a little awkward, but too bad. We all need to get used to this, because I love you both, and we're all family. I'm not going anywhere, and neither are any of you."

I hide my smile. "Okay."

We all sit together and watch the movie. And then Decker comes home from work and also joins us. He and his partner, Nadia, have been working with Felix to see what they can dig up on Olivia. Decker has news for us.

"So Olivia is the mother of Marko's child. The one that Rhett accidentally shot. And I am assuming he is the father of the other baby as well."

"What?" I say as I stand up. This really is all my fault.

Con's eyes widen. "What? You accidentally shot her kid? And Marko, he's the guy that you had issues with? The one who was after Cara?" She turns to look at her sister.

Decker nods. "The kid passed away."

My face goes white. "No, he survived. He was just shot in the leg."

Decker sees my reaction and quickly corrects himself. "No, it had nothing to do with you. He died of COVID, months after the shooting happened. She became mentally ill after that; the grief was too much. Child protective services got involved and took her new-born away from her until she can sort herself out. This happened before she met you, Con."

"But she was at the doctor's, she told me she was eight weeks pregnant," Con says, brow furrowing.

"She lied. She wasn't pregnant at all; she had her baby taken away," Decker explains.

Con shakes her head in shock. "I can't believe it. How did she even know that I was pregnant, though?" She purses her lips, and then her eyes suddenly widen. "I ran into a man at the café near work, and I mentioned to him I was pregnant. He said his name was Marvin."

"Marvin? Or could it have been…" I grit out, my blood boiling at the thought of him being so close to her. He could have hurt her.

She nods. "I think it must have been Marko. Why would Olivia do this?"

"From what Nadia was able to find out, it was more curiosity. She wanted to see who you were, and who you were close with. Maybe she liked being around you because you were pregnant."

"That makes no sense," Cara says.

Decker shrugs. "I'm just the messenger."

Con wraps her arms around me, her small belly digging into me.

I look down at her and kiss her forehead. "I know this is a lot, and I'm so sorry."

She nods. "It is a lot to take in, but we will get through it."

I look over at Cara and she just smiles.

I couldn't give Cara what she needed, and now I know that's because it wasn't her I was meant to end up with. I thought she deserved more than I could give, but it wasn't that. She was just asking the wrong person.

I will always love Cara, but we both grew into different people as we got older. She will always be one of my best friends.

But Con? Con is the woman who holds my future.

And you know what?

It's not that awkward after all.

Cara's right, we're all family.

And that will win out every damn time.

Now that Olivia is in jail and we know why she came after Con, everyone is on high alert. I even met with Temper, the president of the Knights of Fury MC, to discuss the Forgotten Children, and we agreed to stay in contact when it comes to them. Temper and the Knights seem to have a soft spot for Con since she works at their garage, so they're ready to go to battle.

As far as Marko, no one is taking credit for killing him, so I wonder if he's in the wind. If he is, he'll show up eventually and I'll make it my mission to catch him.

Con saving Fire meant everything to the Wind Dragons—everyone is grateful to her and appreciative of what she did. She earned Clover's respect by doing what she did, and that's no easy feat.

We spend the rest of the month selling Con's house and getting ready to move into the new one. I help Con pack up her house. We pull things that belonged to her parents that she'd like to keep, and pack the rest to take to the new house. We managed to find one down the road from Cara, a brand-new two-story house that we both fell in love with. I mean, I would have agreed to anything she wanted, but this house is amazing, with a pool, five bedrooms and two bathrooms.

It's not exactly what I would have wanted, but her being happy is all that matters.

And until Marko is found, it's probably a lot safer than being with me and made a target once again.

And when the time is right, we will move in together.

My number one priority is her and the baby being safe.

Until then I'll be doing a juggling act.

And as for the Wind Dragons?

I don't know where we will end up.

Epilogue

Con

"I have a surprise for you," Rhett says as I'm lying by the pool at the clubhouse getting a tan. I've started coming here every other weekend, just so it's not always him doing the drive back and forth.

"A surprise?" I follow him inside where he has set up a candlelit dinner.

"I'm not the best cook in the world, but I tried," he says, lifting up the lid on the plate and exposing his creation. "Chicken curry, potatoes and steamed rice."

My mouth waters. "It looks delicious. Thank you."

He pulls out my chair, and I sit down. "I hope you're settling in here okay," he says, taking the seat opposite me.

"I'm happy to be wherever you are," I say.

Taking a bite of the chicken, I moan at the taste. "Did you actually make this? Or did you order it and pretend?" I ask him.

He laughs. "Is it that good? I cooked it. I googled a recipe, I can show you as proof." He then takes a bite and nods. "Okay, yeah, actually this is pretty good. I should cook more."

"Yes, you should."

We are quiet for a few moments, enjoying the food and the company.

"I love you," I suddenly blurt out to him. "I've known this for a while, but I've never actually said it out loud. But now we're living together, and having a baby, and we've done everything out of order. But I love you."

He looks into my eyes and smiles slowly. "I love you too, Con."

And then he's out of his chair, and by my side, kissing me. "You're the woman I was meant to be with. You'll be the mother of my children, and my old lady. And I'll give you the world."

I smile, watching him return to his seat.

I feel like this is a perfect moment, even after such a rough week, and I love him even more for it.

And then Bear sticks his head in. "Fuck, that smells good. Is there any more?"

Rhett looks at him like he wants to murder him. "Can't you see we are having a moment here?"

"Want me to play violin?" Bear grins.

Zeke sticks his head in next to Bear's. "Look at you two fucking cuties."

Rhett sighs heavily. "Yes, there is more food; I cooked enough to feed an army. But you can only come and eat after Con and I have finished."

They both disappear, grins on their faces, and I laugh. "I'm not just with you, am I? I'm with them all."

"Love the man, love the club," he says, and I nod.

He's right. If I love him, I have to love all of them.

I have to live and breathe the Wind Dragons, just like he does, and I have to be there for his brothers, just like they are for me.

Loyalty.

Love.

Family.

And I can do that, but I can also love myself and give myself what I need.

Balance, right?

I now have everything that I never did. I've never been so happy that I found Cara's birth certificate, which started this whole new journey.

I might not be a member of the Wind Dragons, but it's still my club.

And my man?

My man is the president.

* * * * *

Acknowledgments

A big thank-you to Carina Press for working with me on this new series!

Thank you to Kimberly Brower, my amazing agent, for having my back in all things. We make a great team, always have and always will.

Brenda Travers—Thank you so much for all that you do to help promote me. I am so grateful. You go above and beyond and I appreciate you so much.

Tenielle—Baby sister, I don't know where I'd be without you. You are my rock. Thanks for all you do for me and the boys, we all adore you and appreciate you. I might be older, but you inspire me every day. When I grow up, I want to be like you.

Sasha—Baby sister, do you know one of the things that I love about you? You are you. You don't care what anyone else thinks, you stay true to yourself and I am so proud of you. Tahj reminds me of you in that way. Never change. I love you.

Christian—Thank you for always being there for me, and for accepting me just the way I am. Thank you for trying to understand me. We are so different, opposites in every way, but I think that's the balance that we both need. I always tell you how lucky you are to have me in your life, but the truth is I'm pretty damn lucky myself. I appreciate all you do for me and the boys. I love you.

Mum and Dad—Thank you for always being there for me and the boys no matter what. And thank you, Mum, for making reading such an important part of our childhood. I love you both!

Natty—My bestie soul mate, thank you for being you. For knowing me so well, and loving me anyway. I hope Mila knows her Aunty Chanty loves her so much!

Sasha Jaya & Aunty Starlyn—I love you both so much! You are the meaning of family.

Ari—Thank you for still being there for me, helping me with my website and anything else that pops up. You are one of the best humans I've ever known.

To my three sons, my biggest supporters, thank you for being so understanding, loving and helpful. I'm so proud of the men you are all slowly becoming, and I love you all so very much. I hope that watching me work hard every day and following my dreams inspires you all to do the same. Nothing makes me happier than being your Mama.

And Chookie—No, I love you more.

And to my readers, thank you for loving my words. I hope this book is no exception.

About the Author

New York Times, Amazon and *USA TODAY* bestselling
author Chantal Fernando is thirty-four years old and
lives in Western Australia.

Lover of all things romance, Chantal is the author of
the bestselling books *Dragon's Lair*, *Maybe This Time*
and many more.

When not reading, writing or daydreaming, she can
be found enjoying life with her three sons and family.

For more information on books by Chantal Fernando,
please visit her website at www.authorchantalfernando.
com.

The Knights of Fury and the Wind Dragons MCs come together in New York Times *bestselling author Chantal Fernando's gritty new series.*

Wind Dragon princess Cara and ex-cop Decker will have to cross every line to be together—including the law.

Read on for an excerpt from Decker's Dilemma *by Chantal Fernando, out from Carina Press!*

Chapter One

Decker

"Why do you always close your curtains whenever I come over?" I cross my arms over my chest and study my baby sister, Simone.

She turns back from fixing the material and plays dumb, twiddling her blond, curly hair around her finger with wide eyes. "I have no idea what you're talking about. It's just sunny out there, and I'm trying to make sure that we don't get skin cancer," she says, blue eyes unflinching.

"I know that your neighbor grows marijuana plants, Sim. And probably more than she is allowed. I wasn't born yesterday."

She purses her lips. "I'm not confirming anything. But if she did, I don't want her to get into trouble. She's a sweet old lady and I'm sure it's medicinal."

I lean my elbows down on her kitchen countertop. "You really think I'd come to visit my sister and arrest some grandma while I'm at it?"

She shrugs. "I don't know. I just didn't want to put you in that position."

"Well, now you don't have to," I say as I move to the window and spread the curtains open, giving me full view of Mrs. Masey's giant plants. "I quit the police force."

"You did what?" Sim asks, stilling. Her brow furrows. "You aren't going to start stripping again, are you? That was awful."

I laugh out loud at that memory. "No, I'm not. Although I still have the body for it," I say as I tap my abs. I used to do a little stripping to make some extra money while I was in the police academy. No one else knows about it, at least I hope they don't.

She throws a tea towel at me. "Seriously, Decker, what are you doing?"

"I've gone to work at Nadia's firm," I explain. "As a private investigator. It gives me a little more control over what I want and don't want to do, and I'm basically working for myself. I thought it would be a nice change."

What I don't admit to my sister is that the line between what the law is and what is right has gotten a little blurred for me. It all came to a head when Nadia was hired to investigate a murder, and together we uncovered that the wrong man had been arrested and convicted. I was reprimanded for helping her and working with the Knights of Fury MC, and my boss told me I would not likely see the promotion I thought I was going to be getting. And after all of that, the fucked-up thing is that I was punished for helping find justice for the victim. If Nadia asked me for help again, I wouldn't have been able to say no. I felt a little frustrated, like my skills weren't being used to the best of their ability.

And if I'm being honest, maybe being a cop wasn't all that I thought it was going to be. I wanted adrenaline, excitement and to help people while getting that rush, but all I got was rules and regulations.

Besides, I don't feel that I was making a difference as a police officer. Not as much as I would have liked. I knew it was time for a change. Maybe I'll regret my choice. Maybe not.

I don't know.

But we will soon find out.

"Private investigation. Isn't that basically the same thing without the badge?"

"Eh. More freedom, fewer rules."

"But you loved putting away the bad guys. You can't do that as a PI."

"Not true. I may not be able to physically put the handcuffs on someone, but I can still help put them away. And I can also help catch the people who aren't necessarily criminals, but are doing something wrong, and that matters more to me."

Sim sits on her countertop, legs swinging, as she gives me an inquisitive look. "I promise I'm not being negative, but don't PIs just catch cheating spouses?"

"You know, that's exactly what I thought when I first met Nadia." I smile at the memory. She had come storming into the station like she owned the place, asking my former partner, Felix, an old friend of hers, for some help on a missing person case. Felix introduced the two of us, and I made a crack about how it couldn't be hard to find out which hotel a cheating husband was at. Nadia shook my hand, her hold strong, while staring me dead in the eye and proceeded to tell me that she was looking for a missing teenager because the cops had given up looking. Her confidence and work ethic made me respect her instantly. "But there's a little more to it than that. And I can choose the cases that I want to take on."

Sim studies me. "It must have been hard, though, for you to walk away from a job you've given your life to."

I nod slowly. "It was."

But I guess I was given a push. If they hadn't caught me helping Nadia would I have stayed? I'm not sure what my answer would be. But my actions have led me here, and I don't have any regrets.

Yet.

"As long as you're happy."

"I think it's the right choice for me. At least for now," I say, glancing around her black-and-white-tiled kitchen. "And Nadia needed someone to help her out, so here I am."

Stepmom life had come a-calling. Nadia went from being a workaholic to being a woman with a family—four children and a partner, Trade. She wanted to take a step back and have a better work-life balance, so when she asked my opinion on taking someone else on, I spontaneously suggested that I might be interested. She was surprised, and asked me a few times if I was being serious. But when I told her it actually sounded like a good idea, she offered the job to me immediately.

"So…what's the pay like?" Sim asks, arching her brow.

"Decent," I reply, realizing the reality of what I did.

"I mean, it's good, it just depends how many cases I take on, which is up to me. Money isn't the issue. I just needed something different. And this is a free-lance job, so I can work as many hours as I like until I figure things out."

I even spoke to Nadia about us upping our prices a little so we can make a higher profit for us both. Nadia is very modest and humble. I'd be charging much more for our services, depending on each case, of course. I'd also be willing to help people out if they needed it, don't get me wrong, but rich people can afford to pay a little more for our services.

"Okay. You are a hard worker, Decker. She's lucky to have you."

"Thanks."

"But you know, if it doesn't work out and you ever need another job, let me know," she teases, smirking as she gets down from the counter, opens the fridge, and scans its contents.

"Thanks, but no thanks." Somehow I can't picture myself grooming dogs with her at her business.

She laughs. "Come on, let's celebrate your new job then. Is it too early for cocktails?" she asks as she opens a bottle of vodka.

I glance at my watch. "Nope."

"Wonderful."

I see Mrs. Masey in her garden from the window, so I wave at her. She spots me, her eyes wide, and then ducks, hiding herself from my view.

I sigh.

At least now no one will be scared of me because of my badge.

"So where did you say you were going? And for how long?" I ask. Sim finally had a chance to hire help at the business, and now she's going on an extended vacation.

"About three weeks. And I'm just going on a road trip. I'm heading east and I'll see where I end up!"

"Well, be sure to be safe, and check in with me every couple of days."

She rolls her eyes. "Yes, Dad."

Simone makes me a Bloody Mary and orders a pizza. We try to get together every couple of weeks, but with the recent job change, it's been a while. We sit down on the couch, talking shit, just like we normally do. We've always been pretty close, and our mom always drilled it into us that we had to look after each other.

When our mom died, all we had left was each other, since neither of us had spoken to our father after he walked out on us when I was ten. So we always make time for each other, even if it's just to check in.

"This Bloody Mary needs less blood and more Mary," I tease, barely tasting the alcohol.

She laughs. "You still have to drive out of here. I think we are too old to be getting drunk in the middle of the day, Decker."

"How responsible of you."

"Responsible is my middle name," she replies, lifting her chin. "The pizza will soak up the little alcohol in there and then you can remain being a functioning adult."

My phone rings, and Nadia's name pops up.

"Hey," I say.

"Hey, are you at the office?"

I glance over at my sister. "Nope, why?"

"We just got an email about a new case. I can't take it—it involves a little bit of travel. Can you take a look and decide if it's something you can swing?"

"Okay, will do."

Traveling doesn't sound too bad. I could use a change of scenery. We hang up and I sign into my work email, scanning the message there.

From: Constance Wilder <cwilder892@gotmail.com>
To: Hawk's Eye Private Investigators
Subject: Find a Person

Hello, my name is Constance Wilder, and I am looking to hire a private investigator to locate my half sister, who I just found out about. I know her birth name, birth date, and where she used to live. She may or may not still be in the Ventura County area.

I'd appreciate your help in finding her. Please let me know if you can help me. Thank you.

Ventura County. Not exactly the holiday destination that I had in mind, but I'd still have to drive over there and stay a night at least while I investigate. Traffic in Southern California is a bitch.

I weigh what I have going on and decide getting out of town wins, no matter what case I have to work. I reply and tell her that I'm happy to help her, and ask if she can send all the information she has.

The job looks easy enough, and it gets me out of town for a few days or so, which sounds appealing after the last few jobs, which were extremely emotionally draining. I'm happy to step away from the corporate embezzling, cheating spouses and petty thefts.

I finish my cocktail with Sim, have some pizza, and then head to the office. This is another benefit of my new job: I actually like it enough that I don't mind going in on a weekend.

I don't know if it's because it's new and exciting, but I love this change, and I'm glad that I followed my gut and took a chance on this.

I'm where I'm supposed to be right now, and it's a good feeling.

My search for a Cara Wilder comes up empty. Constance's email says that Cara is Caucasian and in her midtwenties, that she heard Cara is a teacher, and that she possibly might be using her mother's last name. I search for all teachers named Cara in our surrounding towns and make a list of them. Luckily Cara isn't an overly popular name, and I narrow it down to three people. I do a social media stalk and the first one is a fifty-five-year-old truck driver, while the second is a renowned Black doctor. The third one sticks out to me, not because she's the last option, but because she's drop-dead gorgeous, with shiny long brown hair, wide brown eyes and lips many women pay for.

Her last name is different from both her biological father and mother's, but she could be married. A check with the DMV shows she has the same birth date as Constance's sister. After further research, it looks like she might have taken her stepfather's surname.

Cara Ward.

Even though her social media is private, I learn that

she's a high school teacher, and Constance was right, she lives an hour or so up north. She's been pretty close to Constance this whole time, yet they never knew about each other.

I message Nadia, telling her I'm taking that case and leaving for a night.

Don't miss Decker's Dilemma *by Chantal Fernando, available wherever books are sold.*

www.Harlequin.com